Dreams

A MYSTICAL ROMANCE

Kathy Santaniello

ISBN: 1539058743
ISBN 13: 9781539058748
Library of Congress Control Number: 2016916144
CreateSpace Independent Publishing Platform
North Charleston, South Carolina

*To my husband Peter
who has followed me through amazing adventures,
backed me in my wild ideas,
and never let me forget my dreams.*

*Because of him this story lives.
Born from music, imagination,
and a little magic.*

Preface

Across the churning midnight sea, a mist like no other, swirls and stretches silently toward the small town's shore. A glistening iridescence beneath the full moon's glow – unnoticed, unseen. Reaching the sandy, shell chipped shore, the mist spills outward like a dry, icy fog, shimmering, rolling but continually moving forward. Across the worn cobblestones of Main Street, past the time-weathered shops of the long forgotten fishing port, up the old town's quaint hillside, winding between the houses where the townspeople lay unaware, sleeping. Lost in their own dreams, not one soul has a clue as to what has just drifted into their town.

Cresting the top of the hill, high above the town's shore, the mist rises only to glow more radiantly as it approaches the forest's edge. There, it pauses, moving almost delicately along the edge of nature's dark fortress. Then, pulses of vibrant colors begin to fill the mist as it slowly disappears, inhaled by the forest into its realm of darkness. Though blanketed from the moon's light, twinkling lights begin to dance within the darkness as the mist moves further into the forest's depths. There, protected from the unsuspecting, it will wait.

Chapter 1

*O*n a hill almost forgotten, where the scent of the shore gently caresses the old stately home nestled against the forest's edge, an elderly woman with spun silver hair and regal resignation, prepares.

Abbigale Dupree, denied the love of her heart, remained in the family home after all other family members had gone their separate ways. For it was there that she knew and loved Aaron von Dorne – and hoped that he would someday return. Then one day, Abbigale silently, yet moving with a deep understanding and anticipation, prepared her home. Confident that all was taken care of, she looked at each room as if taking a mental picture to remember it by, then closed each door behind her. With two letters in her hand, she walked out the front door to the mailbox. She put one letter in addressed to her attorney, the other to her niece – Jennifer McBride. Patting the mailbox, she turned toward the house.

As Abbigale gazed at the Dupree home, she also saw her past. All is done, she thought to herself, then with a deep breath, a new sparkle came into her eyes – one of overflowing love – with which she turned, and walked determinedly, and anxiously, into the forest behind the house, never looking back.

Deep in the forest leaves began to rustle. Animals scattered for cover and the birds fell silent. Something had changed. Something, was out there.

Aunt Abbigale Dupree – hers was a sad past. Yet she was Jenny's favorite by far in the Dupree family. Abbigale had so much love to share – always wanted a family, a simple life with the man she loved and the children she hoped to someday give him. When young, she was full of dreams with a deep and strong passion for life. A very gentle woman, with a smile that would cure any wounded soul.

Jenny did not know her Aunt Abbigale back then, though the family often spoke of her youth. Jenny only knew her as her favorite aunt. A beautiful woman even in her later years, Abbigale had an air of almost royal femininity. She always dressed elegantly, although a bit outdated. But it was what was worn in the time she so often reminisced – the time when her memories of Aaron burned the brightest.

Jenny had often been told that she looked remarkably like Abbigale when she was young – petite, with long-flowing dark brown hair, and big eyes so dark and captivating that one would find themselves staring, expecting something profound to be revealed from out of their depths. It was always Jenny's desire to be like her aunt. Looks were not enough. She had always respected Abbigale for her gentle strength and unwavering perseverance. Abbigale was truly a lady of ladies.

Jenny's mother said her sister Abby, her senior by twenty years, only ever loved but one man – "A love we can only dream of." Abbigale's father never approved of Aaron von Dorne. When he found out Abbigale was spellbound in love with Aaron, he forbid her to leave the house without an escort. Her father proceeded to cause so much hardship for Aaron's family that Aaron, emotionally torn by the damage of his love for Abby, was forced to leave for fear of further retaliation. Aaron didn't want any more pain and hardship caused because of him. Poor Abby. Yet Abbigale was not destroyed, crushed. You see, even her father couldn't put out the flame that burned within her heart. After her father died, and all her sisters and brothers had gone to live their lives, Abbigale remained. It was there that she knew and loved Aaron. She had always envisioned him around her. She wouldn't think of leaving.

With a letter from her Aunt Abbigale in hand, Jenny sat back in the worn chair of her small apartment. Some might call it a hole-in-the-wall, but she unfortunately couldn't afford more. Her life was in a shambles. Seems like every time she tried to further herself, she went backwards. Uselessness had been creeping into her apartment the last few days, so much so that it was having an overpowering effect on her. She felt defeated, lost and lonely. She was laid off on Friday from the job she had put so much hope into. Jenny thought about her personal life. It is so personal on one even knows it exists, including me. No, that isn't exactly true, but sarcasm they say is one of the last things to go. Fortunately, we can dump a lot of hurt emotions into sarcasm and no one will know exactly how much we hurt, right? Big cities are known for their bright lights, and something happening everywhere. Fun, parties, shows – the big life! They always talk about the nightlife. What about day-to-day living? What happens when you hardly have enough money to keep a roof over your head? Not to mention morals, upbringing, a decent self-worth, and compassion for those in need and in pain around you. I'll tell you, they don't mix, and if you don't stay strong, you'll slowly, but surely, lose yourself. More and more I long for a gentler, simpler life.

Jenny turned her attention to the letter in her hand. Opening the letter, she caught a faint whiff of Abbigale's perfume, still lingering on the paper. She began to read:

Dear Jenny,

I hope my letter finds you well. I know this may come to you as a surprise, but I am leaving. I have watched you grow up these past years and I see so much of me in you. You have the same basic ideals and dreams as I do. You know this too, that is why we have been so close. I have always believed you to be the daughter I never had, in spirit anyway. Because of this, I want you to live in the house here as long as you wish. I have made arrangements with my attorney to assist you should you choose to accept my offer.

I know these past few years have been difficult for you. A change might do you good. The house is paid for, so you will not be spending your money for rent. The space and air will do you good. Most of all remember, there is love here.

It was signed, "Lovingly, Your Aunt Abbigale." Included at the bottom were the name, address and telephone number of her attorney.

Jenny looked on the back of the letter for a forwarding address. There was none. "Strange. . ." Jenny muttered, "she just must have forgotten. I'll get it from her the next time I talk to her."

Jenny laid the letter against her chest. For a few silent moments, she sat remembering Abbigale's smiling face in the house that she had made a place of wonderful memories for Jenny. Whenever Jenny had visited in the past, Abbigale had always made her feel welcomed and loved. A faint smile rose on Jenny's face, "Maybe moving to the Dupree home is just what I need. I have nothing to keep me here.

4

Actually all my common sense tells me if I don't go, this place will eat me alive – it'll swallow me up without a second thought!" The thought made Jenny shudder, imagining a city with teeth like in Jaws descending over her, with no chance of escape. "No!" she blurted. "There's got to be more for me out there. This isn't life, or maybe I should say living. I don't want to spend my life wasting away, wishing I'd never existed."

Jenny again fell silent in thought. Aunt Abbigale had written in her letter, "Remember, there is love here." I wish I knew what she meant by that. One thing I do know is she loved me. Even if she isn't here, I know I will feel her around me, and right now, I think the security of her love is exactly what I need. Maybe there I will get a new perspective, a purpose – a goal. "Yes!" the word tore past her lips, "I'll do it! Shed this ugly skin, leave it all behind me like a bad dream. There'll be no turning back."

Abbigale often seemed to know Jenny better than she did herself. Jenny trusted her now to know what was best because she certainly didn't know. Her present life showed that quite clearly. "Well auntie," Jenny said, "Ready or not, here I come!"

Chapter 2

*T*he alarm clock rang at 5:00 am. Jenny sprang from her bed with the childlike anticipation of the big move. Her life was starting to change. A renewed flame of excitement began to burn again within her weary soul. "What should I take?" Jenny suddenly asked herself, noticing she had more than would fit in her car. A moment of despair tried to grip her as if to say, "This is impossible, it won't work. Another stupid idea!" No, Jenny thought, let's be rational about this. My lease isn't up for a couple of weeks yet. I'll pack only the things I really need, then the next most important things and so on, until my car is full. I can always come back later for the rest. A forceful, "Bravo Jenny!" erupted from her. "Who said you can't think on your toes?" Having saved herself from that moment of impending doom, she moved more assuredly, with an increasing desire. "All will be ready, complete, by tonight. I will leave tomorrow morning come hell or high water!" she announced with great zeal and exclamation. What she didn't want to admit to herself was the fear that if she wasn't ready tomorrow, she might never be ready. She had to act on this now!

Jenny showered and dressed, singing, "Oh, What a Beautiful Morning," from the musical *Oklahoma*. When she opened the blinds in her room she had to laugh at herself, for the weather was anything but beautiful. Dismal thick darkness, pouring rain, and the wind – it was blowing so hard you couldn't tell which direction the rain was coming from. A damp chill went down her spine. She shivered. "So be that way!" she spewed at the world beyond the window as she dropped the blinds. Turning smartly on her heel, she continued her song even louder as she marched out of her bedroom.

Jenny decided to start her packing in what she figured to be the easiest room – the kitchen. Of course, the fact that she was a bit hungry had absolutely nothing to do with her decision. She had no doubt that Aunt Abbigale would have all the utensils, dishes and pans she would need. Jenny pulled a couple of bags out from under the sink. "First, all the non-perishables," she directed herself. This was done quite quickly. Due to the scarcity of her financial wealth, she was never able to stock much food at any one time. But now, having lost her job, Jenny hardly had any food left in the house. "Now, the fridge." A small grumble awoke in her stomach. "Breakfast nibblies or garbage can, which will it be?" She decided to leave some munchies in the fridge for later that day. "Have to keep up my energy," she chuckled, as she stuffed the remnants of a piece of cheesecake in her mouth.

After finishing the refrigerator, she moved on. All the dishes could stay. It wasn't important if they ever were taken from the apartment. "Can't have too many elegant dinners with plastic-ware now can you? However, they are great for clumsy dates." Jenny smiled and began putting cleaning items from under the sink into another bag. "Just one or two of these. Heaven forbid I should lose track, filling my car with this stuff and not leave room for any clothes. Might get just a tad drafty around the Dupree house, and I don't think wearing cleaning rags will be considered very sporty by the locals in town." Having bagged the items she wanted, she stood with hands on her hips and said, "Two down -- the kitchen and breakfast. Now that's killing two birds with one stone!"

The living room wouldn't take long. Just a couple of pictures, knickknacks, and her portable television. "It may be portable, but darn if it isn't color. I'm not that poor!" she defended herself. The bathroom was next. A real cinch that was. A Tupperware box under her sink held most of the items with one or two small items left over that she threw into one of the kitchen bags.

"Last but not least, the bedroom – no, maybe it's time to take a break. I'm not ready for this one. Besides, it's time for my favorite soap opera to start." Having thoroughly convinced herself, she stopped. The bedroom would take the most time – there was stuff all over it. The morning was almost over. Although it seemed she was tearing through the place, almost half the day was gone. "I'll watch my soap and eat some of the munchies I left in the fridge, then I have to finish my bedroom."

Soap operas are so ridiculously addictive! People watch them every day, some religiously, and for what? Usually you can tell what's going to happen before it does. You can bet there will never be an easy solution to anything, it must be difficult so it will carry on forever, eventually involving everyone, and causing all sorts of devastating repercussions – just like *life*. However, most avid viewers, even with all the craziness, feel it is worth it. The characters become like family. You know everything about everyone. And for just a short time, your ho-hum days or stressing out issues just seem to fade away.

Jenny finished her lunch in front of the television. Once done, she got up and went to her bedroom. Her room wasn't very big. She just kept a lot of things – like a packrat. She went to her closet and pulled down two suitcases from the top shelf. Feeling somewhat embarrassed at the sight of the dust, she joked, "Yuck, if auntie only knew what a terrible housekeeper her niece was she might just reconsider her offer." After getting a better look at the dust on the suitcases, she decided not to open them on her bed as she had originally planned. Instead, she plopped them on the floor and opened them there.

Jenny filled the suitcases with her clothes from the closet, then from the dresser. Her speed slowed dramatically as she began to look at the items on top of her dresser. A picture of her mom and dad smiled lovingly back at Jenny. She recalled, "This picture was taken in their front yard just before they left on their vacation to Acapulco. I remember they had always wanted to go to Las Brisas ever since they saw those pink and white stripped buggies on the old series, "I Spy." This trip would be the honeymoon they never had. Twenty-five years of love, sweat and tears – they barely got off the ground when the plane. . ."

Jenny cradled the picture to her heart as tears escaped from her eyes. "Two years already and I still expect them to come back." Jenny looked at the picture again, having gained some control of her emotions, she smiled at her parents in the picture. She kissed them both, longing to feel real warmth touch her lips rather than the cold lifeless picture glass. Wrapping the picture ever so lovingly in a soft scarf, she laid it gently in the suitcase.

Jenny was an only child. After her parents died, she viewed her aunt to be her immediate family, not just any aunt. Jenny needed to do that, she couldn't accept that she was the last – alone. She had to have someone close.

Next to where the picture of her parents had stood lay a dried rose. Marc Jones, her best friend, gave it to her on her last birthday. Jenny would have stayed home alone that day but Marc, who lived downstairs from her, made it impossible for her to turn down a dinner invitation. Standing in her doorway all tidied up. Shirt mostly tucked in and tie a bit crooked and loose. His brown, wavy hair rustled from most certainly a long day at work of which she was sure he was just getting home from. Then His valiant effort. "You see," she recalled him saying, "I've already spent the money on the food, it's cooking right now as we speak. I started to get a terrible feeling that I had forgotten to do something. Then it hit me, I forgot to invite you – you knew nothing! I feel so stupid. I know it's really short notice, but. . ." his story wasn't very convincing but the look on his face was priceless, how could she refuse? Her self-pity was overwhelmed by his bumbling, boyish attempt of salvaging her birthday. She agreed to dinner. It did actually perk her spirits a bit. But, what made her really feel good was when she looked out the window after taking her shower and saw Marc running back across the street. His arms filled with freshly made lasagna, bread and wine from the corner deli – one long stemmed rose clasped between his teeth. "Boy, what a con artist," she chuckled. Jenny never let on that she knew. He was just a good friend trying to make what could have been a very bad day, a good one – he had succeeded. The memory of her birthday was good after all.

Jenny used to talk to Marc quite often. They were never involved or anything. Their relationship was more like that of a brother and sister. Jenny had always wanted a brother. But those days were gone now, too. Marc's life changed when his company promoted him last month and transferred him out of state. She was happy for him because he was so excited and optimistic about his "moving up in life," as he put it. Jenny didn't have the heart to let him know that she was also very sad at his leaving. She felt loneliness creeping around the corner with the thought of a good friend gone. Jenny dealt with it, though it was much quieter around the place. "I hope you're happy Marc." Having closed that chapter in her life she stroked the rose once – a petal fell.

The room was filled with little things here and there reminding her of moments throughout her past. Along one wall was a long low shelf. It was used as a desk, a place for knickknacks, books, and on one end, she had shoeboxes full of old mementos. Jenny pulled a couple books out which she had always wanted to read but had never found the time for. She tossed them into the suitcase. One by one, she lifted the lids of the memento boxes, rummaging through a little with her forefinger, then closed the lids without removing any of the boxes. Jenny was beginning to look a little perplexed. "Too much junk," she shouted and continued in exasperation, "I just don't have time for it all!" She went through a couple more boxes. She took a postcard of Disneyland – her favorite memento from the trip she took with her parents on her tenth birthday. "Oh, that was a fabulous trip. Mom and dad were wonderful." Jenny liked to remember them there more than any place else. She closed the lid of the last box. They would stay until another time.

Jenny kept a photo album between the shoeboxes. She glanced at it several times while going through her boxes, but elected to ignore it. Now, having finished with the boxes, Jenny felt obligated to pick it up. She handled the album for a while, not opening it. She turned it over several times in her hands. On the front cover of the album it read, "The Life of Jennifer McBride." The words were gold embossed on a background of a beautiful sunset sky, with all the shades of red and orange over a black silhouetted horizon. Jenny received the album on her sixteenth birthday. "What a time of hopes and dreams," she reminisced. She opened the book. The first page had pictures from her party. It was fun. Jenny and a couple of her friends went ice skating in the morning, to the amusement park in the afternoon to enjoy the rides and games, then to top it off, her mother let her take the car to the drive-in for a *girls'* night out. How grown up she felt – in control of her life, and thirsty for more.

It was very late when she got home and her parents had the porch light on, waiting for her return. Of course they tried to look busy with magazines or something when she walked in. Good ol' dad, the one she swore she saw peeking out the window when she drove up said, "You home already? Seems like you just left a minute ago." He couldn't fool her. She had noticed him in the background when her mother turned over the keys. It was a genuine look of sheer panic on his face. He thought for sure that her mother had lost her mind. "You know," Jenny whispered, "some kids are just lucky."

As she turned the pages, she relived moments, sounds and smells of her younger years. The album was just as much a diary as it was a photo album. She made a point of writing down some of her feelings surrounding each event.

Then of course, as with most girls, she was spending more time putting in things about the "boys" in her life. Young loves. . . crushes. . . those tingly feelings you got just thinking about a guy. She had clipouts from school papers and even salvaged photos from the school's photography class trash – one picture was noted, "That's Steve's Hand."

As Jenny got older though, the narratives became shorter and more sparse. As she turned more pages, the pictures, pressed flowers, ticket stubs and such were just thrown in between the pages. Included with these items was usually a scrap of paper with a name and maybe a date or place to jog her memory. Jenny had fully intended to go back and complete the pages, but never did. The items in between the pages got fewer and fewer, until the last used page, which – except for a scrap of paper – could have been like any of the remaining unused pages reserved for some new "love" in her life. Jenny slowly picked up the paper, it read:

Brice – he's the one! I know it!

Jenny crumbled the paper in her fist. The name cut like a knife. Happiness, deception, love, betrayal, compassion, lies. The memories swarmed like stinging bees within her. She tried to blank her mind, to be angry, but it was no use. She couldn't avoid the fragment of deep pain that was hurled at her. A pain she knew if she should ever acknowledge completely might just make her go mad. Jenny slammed the album shut. "This, Jenny McBride, stays here. I'm making a new start, a new life. I can't keep my head up with these memories like weighted chains pulling me down." She put the album back between the boxes, turned around and with a deep sigh surveyed her room.

She had all that she intended to take, except of course for Teddy, who sat very tall on her bed with inquisitive eyes as if to say, "What about me? Don't you want to take me?" Jenny felt a little pang of guilt for not picking Teddy up at the start, so as not to upset or worry him. "Oh boy, a grown woman acting like a two-year-old. What will people say?" Jenny said and immediately continued, "I can see it now. Headlines read:

> 'Grown Woman Cracks – Thinks Stuffed Animal is Alive!
> (Details on page 20, Entertainment section)'"

Regardless, Jenny picked Teddy up, cuddling him close, then with a kiss on his nose, set him comfortably on top of the suitcase.

Jenny was exhausted. It was only seven o'clock, but it had been a long and hard day, both physically and mentally. "I'll put the bags in the car tomorrow morning, then off I go," she said, though in the back of her mind she continued and never again to return.

That night Jenny slept deeply, but not restfully. She tossed and turned into the wee hours of the morning. Uncertainty prowled through her dreams. Jenny had no clue that her life was about to change in ways she could never imagine, or for that fact, believe.

Chapter 3

*T*he Dupree home, now empty, rests in a darkened slumber. Not a whisper is heard within its once bright and love filled hallways. The life-essence almost completely faded now, has somehow aged this once stately home – its grandeur diminished by the force now growing within the forest's depths. The cold darkness within the house is only equaled by the moonless sky outside. All is still. There is a thick silence in the air outside. So strange it would swallow even the hoot of an owl before it left its beak, never to be heard...if there was one to find in this eerie darkness. But now, just beyond the forest's edge, a glimpse of light, twinkling low and soft is watching. . . waiting.

Jenny's alarm again went off a five o'clock in the morning. As mechanical as any robot with a programmed mission, she showered, dressed, and had her car packed before she even mentally woke up. Time – six o'clock. Impossible! she thought. However, the time and facts were correct. She was so excited. She looked around her place one last time. Everything was good to go. Jenny had already disassociated herself from any emotional attachments towards the apartment. She was more than ready. Walking out the door, and locking the past behind her, Jenny stepped out into her new life.

She sped off heading north out of town. The rain from the day before was just about gone. It was down to a light sprinkle. Jenny turned the radio on for some company – driving in the dark can be so creepy sometimes. Her car's movement in the still of the city was so pronounced, almost like watching a flea scurry across the belly of a sleeping dog. That's how she felt in her little Volkswagen bug. She had a strange feeling that if she didn't hurry up, the city would wake up and bite her before she could get away.

Jenny had a tendency to animate and give life to things around her quite often. Her car she named Kit. She got the idea from a television show. Jenny often carried on one-sided conversations with Kit. She actually felt they had a good rapport. Kit liked Jenny – she knew it. She thought it was important to have a good relationship with her car. Heaven forbid she should get mad at Kit, for she knew he would leave her high and dry on some deserted road in the middle of nowhere. Jenny knew many people would say that's silly, but then why do you see other people "pat" their cars? Is there some hidden technical reason? Does it make sure the fenders won't fall off, the dash won't pop up, or the steering wheel won't come loose?

"Come on Kit, let's try that Oldies station and see what they've got playing this morning." She pushed Kit's radio button and he obliged her by sounding out with one of her old time favorites, "California Dreaming." Jenny liked all kinds of music, though she favored the oldies more, mainly because the songs usually stirred up old but good memories. Yes, there were many bad memories in her past, but the time that had passed since these songs were new, made it very easy to be selective of her memories. And let's face it, time has a way of softening and dulling old pains and sorrows. Subconsciously, most people want to forget the bad and remember only the good. That is one of the saving graces that makes it possible for us to go on with our lives.

After little more than an hour, Kit had left the city and was still heading north out through the suburbs with Jenny bee-bopping to the music behind the wheel. Morning was well underway. The rain stopped and the clouds began to fade. A ray of sun suddenly pierced a cloud, flooding Jenny's window with a warm bright glow. She sighed slightly as the sun's penetrating warmth reminded her of being snuggled inside a warm fuzzy blanket.

Jenny felt good. Having in effect shed her past, she felt years younger, energetic and very much alive. She was actually looking forward to the future for the first time in a very long time. With all her excitement, she had forgotten to grab anything to eat or drink. Her stomach grumbled. "I've got to get some more gas anyway. I'll pick up a Danish and some coffee at the same time." The next road sign indicated "gas" one mile ahead. Kit veered off the exit and followed the signs to the station. Jenny was in luck – the station had one of those mini-marts. After pumping the gas, she went inside, picked up a Danish and poured a large coffee, paid for the gas and food, then was back on the road in no time. "That was painless," she commented to Kit, having detoured from their course out of town. "We don't want to waste too much time. We want to get to Aunt Abbigale's early enough to still get some grocery shopping and unpacking done -- maybe even a look at the town -- but at least a few minutes of just plopping before evening sets in."

Jenny's concentration was broken by a song playing on the radio. "Dream Lover," she pondered. Do I even know what kind of man is really right for me? Seems I've been a very poor judge in the past. However, Aunt Abbigale, she knew. She had loved only one man her entire life. Even being wrongly separated from him didn't taint or diminish her love for him. "Aaron von Dorne," she addressed him aloud, then paused for a moment as if picturing him in her mind, "what a man you must have been. What ever happened to you?" She fell quiet and listened as another hopeful love song pulled her back in.

"All I Have To Do Is Dream." It sounds so simple and nice, but you can't live in your dreams or fantasies. Reality has a way of slapping you in the face should you ever try, which I think leaves you feeling even worse, emptier." As the song finished, Jenny changed her focus to the scenery outside.

Fall, what a colorful time of year, yet the beauty is somewhat lessened by the pending cold of winter. "Who knows, maybe winter in the country will be a lot better than in the city." She continued to look at the trees with their brilliantly shining leaves. Many of the leaves had already dropped and were swirling in the road all around her. Some leaves had been caught by the dampness of the ground, where rainwater still clung to the slowly drying surfaces. The air smelled damp, but fresh. In spite of the recent foul weather, it was still quite warm outside. The temperature made the dampness and season changing a little more bearable.

"Ha-a-rses," Jenny blurted in a hillbilly drawl. "Yip," she continued, "must be a Fa-a-rm, I reckon." She giggled at her silliness on seeing the first true signs of the country. "It won't be long now," she told Kit, "and you'll be able to rest your little feeties. Or would you prefer to have them called treads, rubbers, or. . ." a momentary flash of a different meaning of the last word stopped Jenny's list-rattling in midstream and made her blush. "Sure glad no one else is in this car right now. I'd have an awful time trying to explain myself."

Changing the subject quickly, she started talking to Kit – better than herself – about the area in which Aunt Abbigale lived. "I always said it was in the country when I was a kid because I would remember seeing all the trees, the sparse scattering of houses, but most of all, passing farms with all their animals and crops. To me, you lived in either the city or the country. There was no in-between. In reality, the Dupree house is very close to the coast. I just never thought much about the water because I was always so busy visiting with my aunt. I rarely went down to the water, which was on the far side of town from my aunt's house. Regardless of the actual location, I've continued calling it the country. It has a real homey concept, don't you think, Kit?" Of course she knew Kit's answer was in agreement with hers.

Jenny turned her concentration back to the road again. "There's a cut-off from the main road we need to take, Kit. It's not real obvious so we'll have to keep our eyes peeled." A few of the locals got tired of having to drive all the way down into town where the traffic lights and stop signs make any forward progress ridiculously slow, then, have to drive all the way back up this direction just to get to their homes.

So these few locals made what they called a "private drive-through." It was all very hush-hush, being it wasn't very legal and all. They certainly didn't want to rile the sheriff or anyone else. Sheriff Trucker wasn't fooled, though he never said anything. It wasn't as if they had built a new express exit ramp. Traffic would be light to minimal, seeing as how the cut-through only served a small portion of the community.

"If memory serves me right, our turn is about twenty yards after the two-mile marker. It also has a diamond-shaped reflector attached to the base of a big tree. Guess they found it was a bit hard to find in the dark, huh Kit?" Jenny shifted in the car seat, readjusted her hands on the wheel. She started to actually lean forward, straining to see just a little farther down the road. "Soon," she said. Kit's wheels hummed effortlessly as he flew down the road, resurrecting leaves off the road's surface to dance in his wake.

Chapter 4

"Whoa, Kit! There's the two-mile marker." She slowed down, her eyes jumped from tree to tree. "How far is twenty yards anyway? I guess if I see the one-mile marker first, then I've gone too far. You're just too smart for your own good sometimes, Jenny," she said ribbing herself for coming up with such an obvious solution. "There," she shouted, "I see it now!" She turned Kit off the road onto the dirt road. "I hope the dirt is packed down. I'd hate to get stuck in the mud." This was one of those times she was glad to have Kit. He seemed to tippy-toe over the road. If she'd had a big car, she could just picture herself sinking floorboard deep in the stuff. Some of those big cars are so heavy.

Jenny was at the end of the cut-through in no time. Having stopped for a moment at the edge of the trees, Jenny could just barely see the Dupree home at the far end of the road. Her heart jumped. She was even a bit surprised to feel butterflies rising in her stomach. "Jenny, you're acting like a little girl." Jenny drove slowly toward the house. The few other houses on the road seemed to fade in the presence of her aunt's house. A house of its time.

As she drew near, the house seemed to grow larger and more stately, as if trying to show Jenny how protective and safe it would be for her. It would always take care of its own. The house looked almost like new. Beaming white with forest green shutters and trim. It was an architectural masterpiece with all the beautiful sculpting and latticework. If she hadn't had any pre-knowledge of this house, it would almost seem too overwhelming, maybe foreboding. Especially set against the dense forest just a few yards beyond. The yard was immaculate. Overflowing flowerbeds lined the base of the front porch. Up the front steps, a porch swing moved slowly in the breeze.

Jenny parked out at the curb. Abbigale never drove, so she couldn't see any reason to destroy part of the property with a driveway, just to provide others a few less steps to the front door. She had a walkway up from the street – that was plenty. Jenny got out of her car and just looked at the house. An unknown feeling made her pause for some acceptance by the house. She waited for any sense of rejection, but instead felt an inexplicable drawing from the house. She moved around her car and walked up toward the house.

As she reached the porch steps, she realized she had held her breath practically all the way from the car. She gasped. Jenny reached out to touch the first post by the steps. It was warm, pleasantly so. She smiled and stepped up onto the porch. She walked to the swing and ran her hand down the chain in effort to still the swing. It obliged her only momentarily, then slowly resumed its swaying in the breeze. Jenny looked back out toward the street. Kit looked at home. The nearest house was at least half a block back in the direction she came from. Only the forest boasted claim in the other direction. This was the end of the line. That last thought almost made her blood run cold. What if. . . Could it be a Freudian slip? "No," escaped past her lips. "There you go again, making something out of nothing."

She walked off the porch and went around to the back of the house. It was just as immaculate as the front. Jenny turned her gaze toward the forest. An army of trees. "Are they friend or foe?" she wondered, remembering such movies as, *Wizard of Oz* and *Babes in Toyland*. For a moment, she became fixed to that which she *couldn't* see beyond the trees' edge. "Hmm," she quickly exhaled as her gaze broke away.

Jenny took the house key, which Aunt Abbigale gave her many years ago, out of her pocket and went back around to the front door, through the screen, and put the key into the lock. The lock gave her no trouble whatsoever. She turned the key and pushed the door. It swung gently open. Jenny walked inside.

The house was more beautiful than she remembered. The sunlight dressed the room in beautiful colors as it reflected off the crystal lamps by the window. The front room looked like an old-fashioned parlor that had been timelessly suspended in a sandman's mist. She stood and soaked in the smell of the house, stirring old memories before her mind's eye. Times of tears cuddled in Aunt Abbigale's arms. Hot chocolate and marshmallows by the fire. She could almost see her coming out of the kitchen in full conversation, waiting for a response to some whimsical adventure she was sure would brighten Jenny's spirits. Just as she watched the image pass before her eyes, Jenny gasped, feeling Abby's essence wash over her. Tears of happiness began to well. "Home," she thought, "I never knew it before, but now I know it for sure."

Chapter 5

"First order of business is to get my things inside." Jenny almost skipped as she bounced back out to her car. It only took a couple of trips before she had everything inside. "Now, let's see what's in Mother Hubbard's cupboards." She went from the front room back through the dining room to the kitchen. "I'd better make a grocery list, so I can food shop while I'm in town." Her memory reminded her that the first drawer below the counter on the left, used to be the *junk* drawer. "There's bound to be some paper in there," she insisted. Sure enough, paper and pen were shortly in hand. She began perusing the cupboards and refrigerator. All the staples were there as anticipated. Actually, there were more than she had ever used in her apartment back in the city. Therefore, she focused her attention on the fridge. "Looks like mainly fresh vegetables, fruits, and some dairy products will be all I need. The freeze is packed with meats, so it looks like there won't be anything major." She made a list of a few favorites, went back out to the front room, and put the list in her purse. Her stomach started calling to her again. "Unpacking can wait till later. It's all inside, that's good enough for now." She decided it was time to head for town.

Outside, Jenny got into her car, made a U-turn, and headed back down the road towards town. As she drove, she really looked hard at the area for the first time. She was no longer a visitor, but rather a resident. The neighbors would have an effect on her life now. The houses were small, older homes. The area was obviously past its prime, but well settled and cared for. In one driveway, a couple of boys were shooting hoop. Across the way, an elderly lady, sporting a full apron and sunbonnet, was knees to the dirt, grooming her rose bushes and other garden flora. A middle-aged man was painting his fence, while his teen-aged son was working on an old Chevy in their open garage. Everything seemed perfect. The people looked quite nice – the friendly type.

Town was just ahead. The hint of sea air was just beginning to rise from the distance. The town was not very big. It was more like one of those quaint fishing towns you might find driving up the New England coast -- a collage of colors weathered by the salty sea air. Main Street ran right smack through the middle of everything. "I wonder if anyone has ever done a survey on how many *Main Streets* there are in America?"

The General Store was the first Jenny noticed. It must have been the biggest store in town. Not only did it sell groceries, but it had an array of other household goods as well. Next to the General Store was a hardware store, an electrical repair store, an apparel store, and an ice cream shop. On the other side of the street was the barbershop with one of those candy-striped lamps, a local post office, and the Surfside Bar and Grill restaurant, which was attached at the hip to the only motel around – it also boasted the Surfside name. "All Rooms Ocean View," read the marquee. Next to the motel, believe it or not, was a video rental store whose windows must have ached with the neon lights flashing around all the current movie posters. "Looks like some things are becoming more a necessity these days," Jenny said. There were a few more odds n' ends stores on Main Street, but nothing much to mention. Way down at the far end of the street by itself, was a big red brick building, which housed the Sheriff's office and all the various town offices.

Jenny remembered Aunt Abbigale saying that Sheriff Trucker didn't much like being too conspicuous. "That ways you can keep a good eye on things without makin' much ado," he'd said. "A lot less commotion down here at this end of the street," he continued," and with important paper work, detailed plannin' and such, we need to be able to concentrate – for the people's sake that is. Can't have folks just poppin' in 'cause they've nothin' better to do but waste time. Besides, don't wanna make anyone uneasy, thinkin' we was constantly scrutinizin' them, now would we?" Funny character he was, Abbigale professed. But, as a fish is to water, Sheriff Trucker was definitely more the "Lone Prairie" cattle herding type, heading an occasional midnight posse run across the border. He had that John Wayne charm, with an *up-to-somethin'* cowboy twinkle in his eye.

Jenny's stomach roared in neglected pain. Since there were no new restaurants around by the look of things, Jenny turned around and went back to the Surfside Bar and Grill. Before entering, she decided to pick up a semi-local newspaper – which included three other neighboring towns – to see what was happening in the lives of the locals. One can learn quite a bit about who's who just by reading the paper.

Half-paying attention as she walked into the restaurant, trying to glimpse a few headlines, Jenny nearly collided with someone. . . or something, as her startled eyes revealed. The word "sorry" was already passing her lips when she realized she was about to apologize to a tall wooden statue – an old Indian Smoker. She chuckled at herself. "Okay, the least you could do is offer me a menu or something," Jenny's little joke didn't stop the tinge of pink rising on her cheeks.

The restaurant was not crowded, but she really didn't expect it to be with such a crusty weathered exterior. Actually, there were more people than she had anticipated. Must be the last of the good-weather vacationers. Of course some people wait to take their summer vacations after all the kids go back to school, that way they can be pretty much assured of a restful, peaceful time.

A waitress spied Jenny at the door and waived her in, seating her at a small table by the window overlooking the water. Relieved not to be stuck in the middle of the restaurant, she relaxed and ordered a club sandwich, fries and an iced tea. After the waitress left, she opened the paper. Page after page she skimmed for any local town information. There wasn't much. One person in the obituaries, a quilting bee exhibition, and a "Congratulations" article. The article exclaimed the joy of Mabel, the post office clerk, who received news of her daughter's acceptance into Harvard. The article included a picture of Mabel and her daughter. Mabel looked as though her daughter had just been elected president of the United States. This news seemed to be the highlight for the town. "I guess there were no major accidents or traffic jams on Main Street. No activist marches or bank robberies. Just another day in the life," Jenny mumbled to herself.

The waitress arrived with Jenny's meal. Her hunger pangs seemed to be more noteworthy than the paper, for she folded the paper up off to the side and dove into lunch.

Jenny gazed out the window to the shore and the rough sea beyond. Her eyes only returning to take another bite of her sandwich. She let her mind wander. The spray of the surf startled her as it shot over a few large rock formations right in front of her. Here was not a welcoming shore, rather it was a rough, rocky, shell spattered edge where the sea often tossed its debris. The sea here tolerates only so much before it thrusts its anger across the helpless shore. Yet, it is still mesmerizing to watch. Such great power in front of you, like a Pit Bull on a leash. Savage, but contained...for now.

Jenny popped the last fry in her mouth and sat back in her chair sipping the last of her iced tea. Having satiated her stomach, Jenny decided she'd better get on to the grocery store.

Upon exiting the restaurant, she went into her purse to retrieve her keys. Unfortunately, the first probe was unsuccessful. A bit perturbed at the keys, she removed a good handful of purse survival equipment and several papers that were obstructing her search. After removing the papers, the keys were in plain sight. Jenny muttered a few words to the keys for not being there on her first attempt and causing such unnecessary work. She pulled out the keys, then huffily worked the regulars back into her black hole of a purse. When replacing the papers, she realized that one was actually the letter her aunt had sent her. Remembering she had wanted to talk to Aunt Abbigale's attorney, she delayed the trip to the grocery store and headed to the attorney's office down in the city building. It was a nice afternoon, so rather than drive, Jenny chose to walk.

The fresh air was invigorating. As she walked along the street, thoughts of Aunt Abbigale played her mind and memories, like the pins across a music box wheel. She tried to imagine Abbigale when she was Jenny's age. Once that image was in mind, she super-imposed herself over her aunt, as if to somehow better understand Abbigale and the source of her strength, and her undying love for Aaron. Oh, Jenny admired her greatly. "I can't wait to find out where she went. Such a drastic change, leaving the house after all this time. How could she forget to tell me all about it?"

Reaching the building, Jenny looked at the letter again. The attorney's name was Carl Atwood, working out of suite #204. She entered the building. "Why do all city buildings look the same? Do they use the same decorator or supplies warehouse?" Continuing upstairs, she found suite #204 and confidently entered the office.

To the left, typing at a desk, was a woman who could be a twin for Ethel Mertz on "I Love Lucy," and to the right, a few token chairs and greenery had been arranged to offer some semblance of a waiting area for clients.

"May I help you?"

Jenny swung back to the left, not realizing the woman had stopped typing.

"Yes," Jenny said, "my name is Jennifer McBride, I'm the niece of Abbigale Dupree." The woman nodded an acknowledgment of her aunt's name. "I understand Carl Atwood has been handling all the legal matters for my aunt, correct?"

The woman smiled answering, "Of course sweetie, we were hoping to see you come out this way, mainly because your aunt seemed so excited. Please, forgive my manners, my name is Ruth Weatherbee. Carl, my boss, has handled all the legal work for your aunt some thirty years now. She's just like family to us. So, how is your aunt doing?" Jenny looked puzzled. Ruth, suddenly feeling somewhat embarrassed and flustered because she couldn't interpret Jenny's expression asked, "Did I say something wrong honey?"

"Well," Jenny said, "I was hoping you or Mr. Atwood would have heard from my aunt."

Ruth got up from her desk and without losing stride or smile said, "Let me see if Mr. Atwood is free," and promptly disappeared beyond the office door at the back of the room. She returned again, followed by a short gray-haired man in his sixties. A bit robust around the middle, but dressed like a rich Texas oil man, with a stogie in one hand and an expensive shiny rock on the pinky of his other hand, which you couldn't help but follow like a bouncing ball as he talked.

"I'm Carl Atwood, Ms. McBride. I'm glad to finally get the opportunity to meet you." His voice was deep and gentle, yet the air about him indicated he was as sharp as a tack – not a man to be taken lightly. "Ruth here informed me you have not heard from your aunt," he stated, leaning forward quizzically.

"No," Jenny responded, "the last letter I received from my Aunt Abbigale was the one offering me to stay in her house – the one that gave me your address. She didn't mention anything about why she was leaving or where she was going. I thought maybe she was just in a rush and forgot to give me a forwarding address or something."

A deep frown came over Carl's face. Ruth looked at Carl, waiting uncomfortably for a response.

Panic began to grip Jenny. "Okay, what's wrong Mr. Atwood? Don't you know where my aunt is?"

Carl huffed, "We thought for sure she told you. We were waiting for you to fill us in!"

"Oh great," Jenny snipped. "does anyone know where she is? What did she tell you Mr. Atwood?"

Ruth retreated to her chair to avoid any focus in this issue, however, she continued to listen intently.

"Your aunt wrote me a letter and indicated she had sent one to you as well, offering her house to you. I was to make sure all legal papers were transferred into your name. She made some minor changes to her will, which I'd like to discuss with you at a later date if that's alright, and then had me draw up a Power of Attorney for you so you'd have access to the accounts."

Surprised, Jenny said, "What accounts do you mean?"

"Oh, checking, savings, access to her safety deposit box. The Power of Attorney covers anything that might possibly come up."

Jenny felt cold all of a sudden. "I don't think I like the sound of all this. If she's leaving me everything, then what did she take with her?"

Carl acted as puzzled as Jenny felt lost. "It seemed rather strange to me too, at the time. Your aunt, however, assured me that everything was just fine. Everything would make sense to you. . ."

"Make sense to me?" Jenny's voice wavered as she jumped in. "I don't understand at all!"

Carl edged back a step, "Now wait a minute Ms. McBride, please calm down. You didn't let me finish. She said it would make sense to you in due time. All your questions would be answered. I had no reason to doubt her then, and I don't think you should now. She's always been the most honest lady I've ever known. I respect her for that, and you must trust in her word."

Jenny was taken aback. Was this a test? Was there something Jenny should have known, but didn't? "Mr. Atwood, if you should hear from my aunt or anything about her whereabouts, would you please contact me at the house?"

Carl smiled, "I surely will, Ms. McBride." Turning to Ruth, who sat up smartly awaiting his direction, he said "Ruth, pull the file on Dupree and give Ms. McBride the envelope addressed to her." Ruth nodded and went to the file cabinet. Carl turned back to Jenny, "The envelope contains all the legal papers you'll find necessary. I hope staying here will prove beneficial, as your aunt seemed to think it would. Again, it was nice to meet you. I'd like to talk more, but right now I must get back to the case I'm working on, it goes to court tomorrow. Please excuse me." He shook Jenny's hand.

She nodded, still somewhat dazed by the way he sailed over the whole, sticky situation.

"I have the envelope Ms. McBride." Jenny was jolted by Ruth's voice.

"I'm sorry Ruth. . . uh. . . envelope you said?"

"Yes, the envelope with all the papers Mr. Atwood told you about. I will need your signature on a few of the papers though."

Jenny was silent as Ruth pulled out the papers requiring signatures. Jenny signed them without really caring to see what she was signing. She just wanted to get out of there. Ruth pulled the office copies and replaced Jenny's in the envelope before handing it over to her.

"Thank you," Jenny said taking the envelope. Both said rather evasive good-byes, then Jenny walked out of the office.

Before Jenny knew it, she was back at her car. "Kit, where is my aunt?" Fear wanted to take over, but faith in her aunt held the reigns. Jenny tried to blank her mind. "Get a grip Jenny. Everything is okay." Feeling somewhat reassured, she drove off for the grocery store. Half an hour in the store and she was done. All the way back up to the house Jenny would start to ask herself, "But what if. . ." then she'd sharply interject "No!" and again try desperately to remove the thoughts of doubt from her mind. "Okay," she finally said pulling up in front of the house. "This isn't working. I'm going to drive myself crazy. For now, I will accept what Mr. Atwood said, however, I will not stop asking around trying to find out what happened to my aunt."

Finally feeling relief by her decision, Jenny turned off the engine, took her groceries out of the car, and started up the walk. For a moment she looked up at the house inquisitively, then returning her empty gaze back down toward the ground, she proceeded forward and into the house.

Chapter 6

The door shut. Jenny leaned back against it, exhausted. Not wanting to give herself too much time for thought, she readjusted the bags in her arms and went directly to the kitchen. She quickly put away the groceries and silently went back to the front room for her luggage. With suitcases in hand, she went upstairs to unpack.

Timidly, Jenny walked past all of the rooms, being drawn by the light from the master bedroom. Within the afternoon sun were hints of the evening hue. Not gold of day, nor the orange-red of dusk, but an angelic cast of amber light embraced the room, not one corner was left untouched by the glow. An overstuffed canopy bed sat regally in the center of the room, boasting its intricate layers of imported lace around the canopy and skirt. A rainbow of silken pillows crowned the head of the bed, and a handmade quilt lay on the foot. The windows were draped with elegant sheers whose designs shimmered on the walls like stars across the heavens.

Jenny's dreamy gaze now began to focus on the nightstand next to the bed. An envelope was leaning against the antique Baby-Face lamp. It was addressed to Jenny. She recognized the handwriting at once, "Another letter from Aunt Abbigale." Jenny, out of fear or guarded concern, convinced herself to wait until she could sit down to read the letter carefully. Quickly, with the thought of the letter's contents looming over her, she opened her suitcase, put away her clothes, placed her parents' picture on the dresser, and laid Teddy in the middle of the bed. She shoved the suitcases under the bed until she had more time to find a better storage spot. By the time she was finished, the amber light had changed to orange – dusk was approaching. Jenny grabbed the letter off the nightstand and headed back downstairs.

"A nice cup of tea sounds good right about now," Jenny said as she went into the kitchen, while a voice in her head continued to chide her for procrastinating on opening Abbigale's letter. She prepared her tea and decided to drink it on the back steps – ignoring the little voice. She unlocked the back kitchen door and went out. Jenny plopped herself down on the stoop. "Mmm, that really hits the spot," she said taking a sip of her tea. She set the cup on the step and opened the letter from her aunt.

Dear Jenny,

Reading this letter means you have decided to take me up on my offer. I am so happy. You won't regret it.

I know you have probably been wondering why I didn't provide you with a forwarding address. Unfortunately, there will be no way for you to contact me. Because of this, I instructed my attorney to give you my power of attorney. Please use the money I left to you, for I have all that I need. I want you to be able to just concentrate on Jenny. I don't want you to feel like you must get a job before you are ready. For now just relax.

I'm sure by now my whereabouts must seem somewhat of a mystery to you. I just didn't want any interference from friends or any curious neighbors poking around. I certainly don't want to ruin things for you. There really is love here. Just be true to your heart and let it lead the way. Most of all, remember Jenny, don't ever stop dreaming.

*One day soon, you will know where I am — all will be
very clear. I know when that time comes I can trust you to
keep the truth between us.*

Lovingly,

Your Aunt Abbigale

"That is one of the strangest letters I think I have ever received!" Jenny sat there, flipping the letter over and back once or twice, then put it back in the envelope. "I'm not really sure just what to make of it. Maybe a few of her screws finally came loose after all these years."

Jenny looked out across the back yard to the trees that lined the edge of the forest. She strained to see beyond. It was a wall of darkness. "Can't see the forest for the trees." She giggled, "Somehow I don't think that's what they meant by the saying." She continued to look at the forest while she drank her tea, almost as if she expected to see something. It was a beautiful evening. A soft warm breeze brushed her face. Then the air was calm. Silence. An ink poured sky now spread from one horizon to the other, blotting out the sun. One by one, the stars came out of hiding as the moon rose like an ascending silver ship from beyond the forest. Day is done. Jenny took the last sip of tea and went inside.

Back inside the kitchen, Jenny began to prepare some dinner. Every once in a while she would glance out the kitchen window at the forest. Realizing her preoccupation with the forest outside, Jenny ribbed, "What *are* you looking for? Expecting someone? Something?" Okay, now she was really beginning to spook herself. That was definitely not her intent. From that point forward, she avoided the window like the plague.

She took her dinner into the front room. At the far end of the room was a fireplace. It didn't look like it had been used much in the past. It was enclosed by glass doors with fancy brass trim. On the mantle above the fireplace, sat an old-fashioned radio. "I wonder if it works?" Jenny went over and turned the dial on. Sounded just as good as any other radio. A debate arguing the current bills before Congress was in mid-swing. Finding it quite unpalatable, Jenny turned the tuner until she found a light classical station. Satisfied with her choice, she sat down in a corner high-back chair, turned on the table lamp to her right, put her plate in her lap, and started eating her dinner.

To either side of the fireplace were built-in bookcases. As Jenny ate her dinner, she glanced at the books displayed on the shelves. On the bottom shelf, to the left of her chair, were old photo albums and what appeared to be a journal. Jenny put her plate down on the marble side table to her right, and reaching down, pulled out the journal. Continuing to eat from the side table, she began to read through the journal.

The cover was surprisingly plain. Just a worn, padded, deep green leather. Inside the cover, on the first page, was Abbigale's name and birth date. The first entry was made on the following page. Abbigale was just eighteen. She wrote of her birthday, the presents, games, and delicious foods that were spread for the occasion. She also talked quite endlessly about Aaron.

Their romance happened rather suddenly and unexpectedly. But Abby was quite smitten from the moment she laid eyes on him. Seems he was new in town. One of her other friends had just met Aaron and invited him to tag along, since most of the young people in town would be there. Abbigale described the moment she saw him as if, ". . . the world had stopped in place for a moment, then whirled forward again in a kaleidoscope of beautiful colors and mind drugging sounds. Yet. . . all I could see were his deep burning eyes that held my heart like a dove. My knees went weak, my face flushed. . ." From the sounds of the journal, the feelings were mutual. Evidently, Aaron stayed pretty much at her side for most of the day. Jenny turned more pages.

The next entry that caught Jenny's eye was about two weeks later. Up to that point, the journal talked mainly about Abbigale's relationship with Aaron. However, this particular entry started with the word "Father," which seemed out of place. As Jenny read, she began to feel very sorry for her aunt because it was obvious Abby's father was beginning to interfere and cause problems for Aaron. While passing her father's office door one day, Abby overheard him quietly insisting to his attorney that, "Something must be done with this boy, this outsider. He's not the right caliber for my daughter. Your investigation proves that."

Abby was crushed. She had to meet with Aaron that evening in *The Place*, as they called it. They didn't talk much. What could be said to undo the things her father had done already? Aaron loved Abby too much to try to make her turn against her own father. They just held each other close, in silence, comforting each other just by being there. Abbigale's retelling of their meeting poured with intense emotion. A few words had been spoken in *The Place*, but the words she would remember for years to come were when Aaron said in parting, "Abbigale, I don't know what will come of all this, but believe in my words. You are my love – my life. Someday I do believe we'll be together again. I don't know how or when -- I just feel it. I can't say why, but for some reason. . . here, right now. . . I believe it with all my heart." Abby loved and believed in Aaron. His word was good enough for her.

The entries following that day were strong and hopeful. Even the entries after Aaron was forced to leave, were just as those before. Jenny was amazed. Her aunt truly believed Aaron and she would be together again. She had undying faith in his word.

Jenny stopped for a moment to think about their relationship for a while. To be able to believe in a man so completely, no matter the circumstances around you, the feeling must be indescribable – or heavenly, maybe. Jenny was moved by the passionate way in which her aunt wrote. Abby's feelings and emotions were felt by Jenny as if she were experiencing them herself.

As Jenny turned the pages, many words stood out from the paper - Aaron, love, *The Place*. Abbigale took regularly to long walks in the forest, though it was more a guise so she could spend time at *The Place*. She would stay there and daydream for hours, remembering all the times they shared, so, so, long ago.

The years passed as the pages turned. Abbigale was steadfast in her love for Aaron. The journal became more a collection of letters to him, as she spoke to him daily – on paper.

More words, "hope you are well. . . I love you, Aaron. . . I dreamed of you today. . . *The Place* is still as beautiful as ever. . . I can't wait. . ." Jenny was gradually getting tired as she skimmed what appeared to be repetitious entries in her aunt's journal. She closed the journal not wanting to read further. Maybe some other time, but it was late and it had been a very long day. Jenny put the journal back on the shelf and took her dishes to the kitchen. The thought of cleaning anything made Jenny's body wither. Her energy draining rapidly, she left the dishes for morning and slowly dragged herself upstairs to bed.

Feeling like a little girl in the overstuffed bed, Jenny turned facing the windows and cuddled her bear, Teddy, close beside her. She lay there in the dark, save for the moon's milky glow that descended through the open sheers. Beyond the windows, she could see the forest. Jenny's eyes glazed over in a glassy stare. Motionless, she watched until her mind drifted, succumbing to the Sandman's call.

As Jenny slept, her mind flew past clouds of decaying memories. Some new, some old. It was an emotional rollercoaster as each scene transgressed from one into yet another. Happy, sad, all the good and bad. The memories changed without discretion. If anything, maybe sadistic humor at best. Nonetheless, changing without allowing any rest. Finally, her mind tired of the pace, settled down into a dream.

The breeze from outside Jenny's window blew across her face and stirred her dream. She was running in a white flowing gown through dimly lit halls of an old aging castle. The wind swirled, whipping hair into her eyes and making it difficult to see. She was lost, afraid, and so cold! She ran and ran, stumbling over shadow covered spurs in the stone floor. Her sleeping world grew darker and darker. She couldn't ignore the growing feeling that someone, something, was watching, waiting, anticipating. Fear – jolted Jenny awake.

Realizing her cold feeling was from the breeze outside, she got up to close the windows. As Jenny latched them shut, something in the woods caught her eye. She peered out beyond the glass, leaving the last window open just a touch to catch any sounds. The breeze began to sound more like whispering voices.

Jenny looked to the left and right ends of the forest. She looked over the tops of the trees. Her eyes tried to probe the darkness of the dense forest. "Where is it? Maybe my mind is just mixing things up. I was just asleep after all. Maybe my eyes became aware of the stars but just displaced them, making me think the light was coming from the woods? Or am I just imagining things?" Jenny said uneasily. Not seeing anything as yet, her ears strained at the breeze trying to decipher the whispers. Then. . . nothing. Complete silence. Jenny held her breath. Drip. . . drop. First one, two, then a gentle sprinkle began. Rain. Jenny shivered, then closed the window the rest of the way. She remained at the window still looking for something tangible to calm her imagination. There must be an explanation, she thought. Rain continued to fall. The view began to be obscured as each rain-drop scurried down the window, finally creating a blur of indefinable images. Jenny strained harder, but it was no use. Like a child's watercolor left out in the rain – everything ran together as one.

Jenny sighed, then returned to bed. She snuggled a little deeper under the covers and nuzzled Teddy a bit closer. Without thought, she began to whisper her bedtime prayer she often recited when she was a little girl. As she grew up, she only seemed to remember it when she was scared or lonely. She felt calmer after she'd finished. Jenny lay there thinking about the forest. "What is it about these woods? I keep finding myself looking at them for no reason! Tomorrow. I'll take a walk out there tomorrow." Satisfied, she closed her eyes and drifted into a gentler sleep.

Chapter 7

Jenny awoke to the sound of birds chirping outside. She felt quite toasty with the morning sun warming everything it touched. She hated to move, it was so cozy. She lay there for a while, feeling pretty good about herself and the choice she had made to move from the city. Finally, reluctantly, she swung her legs out from under the sheets and sat up on the edge of the bed. She sat there silently while the few remaining fragments of her dreams faded into obscurity. Then Jenny remembered the forest. She went over to the windows and opened them wide.

It was a beautiful morning. The air was brisk, refreshing. She looked out across the yard to the forest. Everything was as it had been the day before. No unusual transformations in the night. "Time to get started," Jenny said as she turned back around to the room. "I'm so excited, " she said taking a moment to relish in her feelings of happiness. "Thank you so much Aunt Abbigale." Having shared her gratitude with her aunt's spirit at least, she made up the bed, tidied the room, then headed down the hall to take a shower. Was it possible for even the shower water to feel cleaner in the country, she questioned herself. After she was finished in the bathroom, Jenny went back into the bedroom to get dressed. Something suitable for tromping in the forest. She pulled out a pair of blue jeans, a flannel shirt, and tennis shoes.

Once dressed, Jenny bounded downstairs to the kitchen. She put on some hot water for tea. As the water began to warm, she cleaned up the dishes from the night before. Just as the tea water started to boil, she dropped two slices of bread into the toaster and pulled out some raspberry preserves from the pantry. Jenny poured water into a mug with a tea bag. The toast popped. She promptly buttered the toast and spread on some of the preserves. She stood at the kitchen window gazing outward as she devoured her toast and tea, not letting her mind concentrate on any one thing. Once finished, she cleaned up her breakfast dishes and decided that the rest of her unpacking was the responsible thing to do before she went off to play. However, her true desires showed through by her haphazardous effort.

When Jenny felt she had sufficiently settled herself, she knew she was ready for her adventure into the forest. She felt much like a kid again as one or two butterflies tickled inside her with anticipation. Why was she so excited she wondered. It was just the forest in back of the house. The thoughts of last night still lingered with her – a possible understanding hovering just beyond her mental grasp. Then she remembered Aunt Abbigale, how would she recognize her special place? The forest was vast. Nevertheless, Jenny was confident. Quite sure she would feel it when she was near – like some psychic aware-ness. Maybe she would hear her aunt – remembering how the breeze last night sounded like actual whispering.

Jenny had always been in awe of the complexities of the mind, and the possible capabilities we can only speculate about or wantingly acknowledge as fact. She often hoped she would be used as a catalyst for such a gift. Maybe. . . "Get a grip Jenny," she blurted out. Feeling a little foolish, knowing how a good majority of people believe such thoughts are evil, anti-religious, or even blasphemous in a way. How could using your mind to its fullest potential be anything but wise – as long as it was used in appreciation, with good moral conviction, and to glorify our maker who bestows such gifts? Oh well, she thought. If she continued on that same track, it could be hours before she went anywhere. Jenny often sat and contemplated such things. "I need to look at the forest without any more delay," her words having somewhat surprised her, declaring a *need* to see the forest.

Jenny went out the back kitchen door and began walking toward the forest. Feelings were all she allowed herself to experience as she approached. She felt like a weather vane in a turbulent storm the way her feelings flip-flopped back and forth, making 90 to 180 degree turns without a moment's hesitation. First, she saw the forest as if under a microscope – wood, leaves, insects – one of many such forests on this planet. The next moment she saw the deep beauty that God had created, looking at it as if seeing a forest for the first time. Then she would see hidden meanings, revelations, animation, and intellect within each fiber that existed there. Jenny was definitely in search of something. . . but what?

She had walked through many forests in her past, none of which moved her in any noticeable, purposeful way. Wanting to be very logical or rational about it, Jenny tried to evaluate whether her reactions were more motivated because of her current emotional, life position. Maybe she was subconsciously reaching out, hoping for something that could make everything better.

Jenny slowed as she neared the wooded threshold. She felt very small and unimportant next to the tall majestic towers of nature which stood silent before her. She stopped briefly in reverence as if the age of the ancient timbers held a vast wisdom of which she longed to one day share. Then, she stepped between the trees, fading into the shadows – no longer visible from the house of the Dupree family. She was now a part of that landscape which she had pondered since her arrival. It had seemed to be growing within her – but now she was within it.

Chapter 8

*J*enny walked in silence. Her senses seemed to be alive for the first time. Smells, sounds, everything filled her, moved through her as if cleansing her soul. It was very draining to stay at such a heightened sense of awareness. The cold stone slabs of the city had taken so much from her. She began to understand that part of what molded a person was their surroundings. They are a part of you. It is much wiser to be surrounded by a living menagerie created by God than entombed, in the cold, lifeless maze of concrete erected by man, to sustain his perpetual greed for power and wealth.

Quickly looking for a place to catch her breath, Jenny sat down on a fallen log. The emotions of the moment swelled within her – finally ebbing – leaving her purged of many past frustrations and pain. Like breaking a fever, Jenny began to feel more alive. She was beginning to heal.

Feeling somewhat dazed after her climatic inner rejuvenation, Jenny began to walk aimlessly, yet deeper into the forest. She was aware, but numb. As if in a trance, she walked as if beckoned toward a misty glow in the distant forest. She didn't try to analyze her decided movement, much like the fish who unquestioningly accepts his journey back up the river, knowing he might never return from what fate awaits him there.

Beautiful white lilies. So brilliant! Until now, time seemed so obscure beneath the dense forest green. But now, a doorway to the heavens opened in front of her. The sun reflected off the lilies, and shimmered endlessly through the airborne particles of Mother Nature, creating an almost pastel-pink hue. Everything looked soft, delicate. It was exquisite! Two song birds circled and looped playfully within the forest break as if protected in a huge invisible birdcage designed by God. It was so different, quite unlike the rest of the forest.

Jenny was almost afraid to breathe. Afraid she had stumbled onto sacred land – unworthy of entrance. Timidly, she moved forward toward a welcoming moss encircled rock, in the center of the break. The moss flirted little violet colored flowers the size of baby's breath. Even the rock seemed inviting. It glistened and sparkled under the sun's attentions. "Fool's Gold I believe they call it," Jenny recognizing some of the rock's content, but it also appeared to have veins of crystal white agate. She had never seen anything quite like it before.

Standing at the edge of the flowering moss, she felt compelled to remove her shoes – fearing she might damage the plant otherwise. The moss was so plush. Her feet gently dipped in the thick green expanse. A feeling of euphoria overcame Jenny, enticed partly by the exhaustion her senses felt having succumbed to her recent emotional surges.

The thought of rehashing her responses to everything around her was too taxing. Rest – the thought entered Jenny's mind as if blown in by a breeze. The sun was warm, enticing. She lay next to the rock, on the flowery moss, caressed by the sunlight above. She took a deep breath. As she exhaled, she felt like butter melting into the world around her. As Jenny drifted, she thought she heard a familiar voice saying, "Time to be who you want to be. Time to go where you want to go. What is hope, is reality. What is desire, is true love. What is dreamt from the heart will always be forever." Jenny's mind drifted on.

Jenny tried to focus her thoughts, but her mind refused her urging. Rather, it chose to frolic through the awakened sensations – real, newly found truths – moving – life-satisfying. She felt untainted. Nothing could touch her. She was not a part of *that* world anymore. She felt as if new beginnings were just at her fingertips – ahhhhhh – her mind shifted to neutral, drifting peacefully – tranquil. The sun's warmth charged her with new life, energy. The desire to sleep, to dream, began to call to her. Just as she was ready to surrender to the call of the dream world. . . "What time is it?" Jenny's internal clock pulled her. Unwillingly Jenny roused just enough to look at her watch. "My goodness!" Her conscience plummeted back. "It's getting late. I must head back. There are so many other things I need to do today. Another time. I'll come back another time."

Jenny saddened – feeling like she was saying goodbye to a dear friend forever. She felt a deep attachment to this place. As she forced herself to get up from the flowery, moss-softened floor, she caught a glimpse of the other side of the rock. To her pleasure, she spied a glistening, crystal-clear pond. It actually made her thirsty just to look at it. Like a mirror, it was. So clear and pure, it could reflect one's soul. Upon dipping her foot into the water, Jenny found she could distort light, motion, and time all in one swoop. Jenny grasped a handful of water and threw it halfway across the pond before it could vanish between her fingers. As the water droplets touched the surface, the pond began to light up like a thousand sparklers. This is indeed a wonderful place! Jenny thought. I must come back here again when I have some time to kill.

Jenny stood and took a slow panoramic look at all the beauty around her as if to permanently imprint it into her memory. Not just the sounds and smells, but the actual picture. As her eyes moved slowly, purposefully from one sight to another, she began to hum a little tune. Her eyes began to move more quickly – her humming louder. Spinning once around, then twice. Around and around she went. Faster and faster. Louder and louder. Until she was spinning in circles, head back and arms stretched out in the air, music flowing from her body. "Yes – this is a wonderful place!" Realizing her silliness, she slowed to a stop. "I must go now."

Jenny left quietly so as not to disturb the tranquility of the place. As she stepped out of the clearing back into the surrounding thick darkness of the forest, she spun around, afraid the clearing wouldn't be there. She felt it calling her. Reluctantly, she turned away. Soon she was surrounded by the towering trees and undergrowth. No sign, not a trace. "Was I really there?" She paused a moment, "Yeah. . ." With a smile, Jenny walked back through the forest, finally emerging onto the grassy expanse at the back of the house. She turned once back toward the forest in remembrance of the beautiful place, then quickened her pace towards the house as she began planning the rest of her day.

Chapter 9

*T*he Dupree house was rather secluded. There were houses only on the one side of the road, which made the front view from the house quite serene. Most of the townspeople either knew Abbigale or at least knew of the Dupree home and family history.

Jenny began thinking about the mysterious events surroundings her aunt's departure. She had already talked to Abbigale's attorney – proving quite fruitless, unfortunately. Maybe Abbigale's neighbor, in the next house could give her something better to go on. Jenny came in the back door from her jaunt in the forest. She buzzed into the front room to check her appearance in the mirror over the fireplace. A little messed, but nothing a few fingers couldn't smooth out. Looking a bit more presentable, Jenny walked out the front door and headed toward the corner of the porch, where she did a quick scissors over the railing onto the grass. Without missing a step, she briskly walked toward the neighboring house.

Some people can be very persnickety about their yards. With this in mind, Jenny kept towards the curb as she neared the house. Besides, she wanted to see if there was a name printed on the mailbox. She was in luck. The mailbox boasted the name "M.A. BAXTOR" in bold wrought-iron letters atop the box. "Okay, so you are the Baxtor's. Or maybe it's just one Baxtor. Separated, divorced, widowed, or maybe a spinster like my aunt. Of course, it could be a man. No, I think I would have heard something about it if there was an eligible man living next to my aunt. Any elderly man would be crazy not to try to make a move or two on her – she was so beautiful.

The Baxtor home was not as grand as the Dupree home. Instead, it was rather quaint. A small, deep-red Cape Cod style house. Jenny stepped up to the door and rang the bell. After a moment, the door opened, releasing the smell of freshly baked bread.

"Mrs. Baxtor?" Jenny inquired of the elderly woman standing before her.

"Yes? Can I Help you?" she replied.

"My name is Jenny McBride. I'm Abbigale Dupree's niece – the elderly lady who lives next door to you?" Jenny added as she saw the lost grimace on the woman's face.

"O-oh, yes. I'm so sorry. I never quite got around to meeting her," she began apologizing to Jenny, "You see, I just did move in last month, and well, I was meaning to get over there, but, well. . . I guess. . . I feel just awful."

"What do you mean awful? You needn't get worked up over it, just because you didn't talk to her before she moved away."

"Moved! Dear child, I thought something tragic had befallen her."

"Now what would ever give you an idea like that?" Jenny tried to keep her calm with the woman, but she could feel the concern mounting within her. Obviously, old woman Baxtor saw the concern in Jenny's face, realizing maybe there was some doubt. "Come on inside, we'll talk a spell." Mrs. Baxtor motioned Jenny on in to the couch, "I'll get us some tea. Nothing like a warm cup of tea to lift your spirits."

Why did she have to say spirits, Jenny thought, now I'm starting to get the creeps. "Calm down Jenny," she whispered to herself, "it's probably nothing. Old woman Baxtor is just a little nutty, or senile."

Jenny couldn't completely shake the feelings, even as Mrs. Baxtor returned with the tea. You see, deep down Jenny knew something wasn't right. Things were not as they seemed.

"Well Jenny, have you come to live with your aunt?"

Jenny's eyes popped. Boy was she out in left field. Did someone leave her out in the rain or something? Jenny felt a bit embarrassed for thinking ill of the woman, for she was rather sweet.

"Uh, n-no," Jenny blurted. Leaning forward she continued, "Actually, I'd like you to tell me more about the comment you made. Why did you think something "tragic," as you put it, happened to my aunt?"

"I'm sorry dear, it's just the babblings of an old woman."

"I'm sorry too, Mrs. Baxtor, because I think maybe there's more to it than what you're saying. Please, I'd like you to tell me anything you know about my aunt. To be very honest, I've had my doubts. I don't feel comfortable with the way things were left. The whole idea of my aunt even leaving her home is so totally out of character for her. To top that, no one seems to know where she is!"

Mrs. Baxtor's face mirrored the same feeling of doubt that Jenny had been trying to suppress. "Well," Mrs. Baxtor started, pausing to take a sip of her tea. Jenny eased back into the couch so as not to seem too overpowering. She also began to drink her tea, but not once did she take her eyes off the old woman. Jenny sat very quiet and listened as Mrs. Baxtor spoke.

"Like I said, I never did actually meet your aunt. Why, living right next door you can see someone every day and never even talk to them. A second or two in the morning, another in the late afternoon. You see? Oh my, here I am starting to babble again."

"Please go on, Mrs. Baxtor," Jenny urged.

"Oh, yes, yes. Well, I never saw her outside too often except her daily trips to the mailbox. I saw her go in and out her back door a couple of times, but I'm not sure just where she had been or what she had been up to out there. Nothing much to talk about. I never saw her just sitting out on her porch, anything like that. Until. . . "

"Until what Mrs. Baxtor?" Jenny prodded her on.

"I guess it was back a spell, not too long ago though. I saw your aunt at the mailbox putting in a couple of letters. She was looking long and hard at those letters. You could tell she was thinking real serious there. She finally put the letters in and closed the mailbox. But rather than walking back to the house, she just stood there looking straight at her house. I was certain something important was on her mind. She had a kind of faraway look on her face. Now mind you, I might be a trifle old, but I've got good eyes – never failed me yet. I was getting a bit tuckered out standing there, just watching *her* standing there. Land sakes! I thought if she didn't move soon, she'd surely sprout roots or something! I didn't want to stop watching. Guess it was one of those funny feelings you get at times, when something is peculiar? Well, just as sure as I had seated myself on this couch where you are now, she started walking back. See Miss McBride, you can see the mailbox right out this window."

Jenny turned and looked, nodding her head in agreement. "So my aunt went back into her house?"

"No, no child. Just like you, I figured she would, but she was heading towards the back of the house. I got up and quickly went to my kitchen window. There she was, walking straight past the house. Standing real tall. Walking at a speed of a woman 30 years her junior. Like Muhammad going to the mountain, your aunt was headed right for the forest – with a purpose! I watched until the forest shadows encompassed her. And that dear Jenny McBride, was the last time I ever saw her. Mind you, I didn't stay at my kitchen window all night, but I did take a peak every so often to see if she was walking back to the house. At times, I even checked to see if the lights in the house were on – in case she had returned when I wasn't watching. I mean, you know I do busy myself with other things around here. I don't just snoop after people." A pale flush came over her cheeks as she realized what a busybody she must have appeared to be.

"Wow, that doesn't make much sense," Jenny said, unaware her thought had slipped past her lips.

"I know," the old woman retorted. "But from what I saw, you do see how I came to my conclusion, don't you?"

"I suppose so," Jenny said hesitantly, trying to mull over all this new information.

"Didn't you say your aunt had moved away, though?"

Jenny merely nodded, for the gears in her brain were churning far too much to allow a verbal response.

"Well now, you see? Everything must be okay. Your aunt just came back when I wasn't looking. Just like I suspected." Mrs. Baxtor tried to smile confidently at Jenny. It was obvious that Mrs. Baxtor was sorry she had said anything to Jenny about her aunt. She was becoming a bit restless.

"I want to thank you for the information. I really do appreciate you taking the time to talk with me – really I do." Jenny tried to emphasize in an attempt to relax the old woman. "Guess I'd better be going." Jenny headed to the door. Mrs. Baxtor hurried to open it for her.

"Now I'm sure you'll be hearing from your aunt soon. Try not to fret so much, it'll all be just fine."

Jenny headed back to the Dupree home. "Okay Aunt Abby, which is it? A departure or disappearance? I'm not so sure about anything anymore. I came out here to get my life back together and seems as though I've landed in the middle of a mystery." Jenny was silent the rest of the way into the house.

Chapter 10

Jenny was famished. She went into the kitchen and fixed a sandwich. Not wanting to waste the time in setting it out proper on the table, she just leaned over the kitchen sink so as not to drop crumbs all over the floor. As she woofed down her food, she found herself staring at the forest. A smile crossed her lips just before she took another bite of her sandwich – she was thinking about the place she had found in the forest. But now, looking at the dark and thick edge of the forest, she wondered if the place really did exist. How could such a place be? Surely, it should be overrun by all the other growth around it. Yet, it was there, as if some caretaker took great pride in nurturing the creatures and life that lived and grew there. "Maybe it wasn't quite as I remember it. Let's face it. After being in the deep wild of an untamed forest, any clearing would probably seem to be more than it was." Jenny's mind drifted for a moment, her eyes becoming fixed, but unfocussed.

Shoving the last bite of sandwich into her mouth, Jenny cleaned up what little mess she had made. "I've got to get my head going in a positive direction for a change." Jenny tried to push back her thoughts up to this moment, and start working on *improving* her life. She wasn't doing anything to better her future and – isn't that what Aunt Abbigale wanted? Wasn't that the whole purpose behind moving into the Dupree home? Aunt Abbigale certainly wouldn't have wanted Jenny to spend all her time worrying about her whereabouts. Jenny's eyes brightened,

"Maybe this confusion was on purpose. Maybe, just maybe, Aunt Abby isn't ready to say where she is. Wouldn't that be a kick." Jenny chuckled at the possibilities.

"Okay, so enough of that! At least for now." Jenny was now pacing back and forth. Finding the kitchen size a little restrictive for her mobile thinking pattern, with a huff, she adjourned to the front room that would surely be more conducive to thinking.

"First things first. I think I'd like to get to know the people around here a bit better. So how do I get myself involved?" A deep furrow appeared on Jenny's brow as she pondered her dilemma. "I know," she said as she stopped dead in her tracks, "I'll go into town to see if any of the waterfront shops need any help. Part-time would be perfect. It's not like I need the money right now, but the 'P.R.' and little nest egg I can get from a job would be great. Maybe I might even meet some people my age." With the thought secure in her mind, Jenny left the house and headed into town.

As she turned onto Main Street, Jenny looked for a place to park, somewhere middle of the block, she hoped. Just as she was about to give up hope, a car backed out of an angled spot. Jenny quickly pulled in. She looked in the rearview mirror and decided to brush her hair and throw on a little lipstick. "I'll be inconspicuous. I want to check it all out first before I let anyone know I want a job. If I see something interesting, I'll come back tomorrow, more appropriately dressed."

Jenny walked along the storefronts looking for signs in the windows. *Help Wanted* was usually easy to see, but sometimes owners would display signs that looked more like solicitous flyers. Jenny wanted to make sure she didn't miss a one. The General Store needed a stock boy, the Surfside Bar and Grill needed a waitress. There was a catalog outlet store looking for "18-year-old with vehicle." "I'll bet that's for deliveries and maybe even worse - distributing catalogs. No thanks!" Jenny continued looking. At the end of the block on the ocean side of the street, there was a bookstore which she hadn't noticed her first time through town. As she neared the store, she read the words stenciled on the front window:

"OFF THE WALL BOOKS
A selection of rare and hard to find books"

In the bottom corner of the window stood a sign written not in the usual bold print, but in fine calligraphy. It read:

"Reap the benefits
from the unusual.
-Inquire within- "

Well that certainly piqued Jenny's curiosity. She decided to go in and browse.

Opening the door, a small bell rang above her head. She stepped inside. It smelled musty. The building was obviously old. The floor was covered by faded wooden slats. The walls, ceiling, everything, was wood. A center pole supporting a second level was made from an actual tree, just trimmed and skinned, then treated so as not to rot. Bookcases lined the walls and several racks stood evenly spaced across the floor. Jenny walked down one of the aisles towards the back of the store. A big window sliced the dark corner with a view out to the ocean. The light from the window cast an eerie glow on the room. A desk stood in front of the window. Seated behind the desk was a weathered looking old man, nose deep in a book.

As Jenny approached, the man remained unmoving. Deep lines etched his tanned face. His silver wavy hair stood out against the navy blue turtleneck he was wearing. The smell of coffee and cherry pipe tobacco now began to tickle her nose.

"Hello," Jenny said. Still nothing from him. Reaching the desk, she laid her hands on the front edge. It obviously broke his line of vision and concentration for the man snapped to, then quickly fumbled with a hearing aid that had been set off to the side.

"Oh, I'm sorry. Have you been standing there long? Without this hearing aid I wouldn't even know a swarm of bees had surrounded me until they stung me."

"No, I just came in." Jenny replied.

"Well what can I do for you, little missy?" He sputtered out before taking a sip of his coffee. "Can I interest you in some books?"

"Actually, I saw your sign in the window – the "Reap the benefits. . ." sign - it said to inquire within."

"Oh yes, I'd almost forgotten about that sign. This is such a small town, hardly anyone asks about it. I put it there because I'd like to start doing some more fishing. I've been getting a bit claustrophobic sittin' here all week. Don't get me wrong, Miss. . ." he paused, waiting for Jenny.

"My name is Jenny McBride." she responded.

"Well, I just decided it was time to get some help in my store. You wouldn't be interested would you?"

Jenny was caught by surprise. So much for being inconspicuous. Jenny blushed saying, "Uh. . . I guess. . . well. . ." she continued to stammer.

"Spit it out girl. Are you or aren't you?"

"I'm sorry, I wasn't ready to outwardly solicit," as she tried to smooth her hair with her hand. The old man laughed catching on to her situation.

"You're not from these parts are you?"

"No, I've lived in the city for many years."

"I'll bet you were planning on coming back here all prim and proper, best foot forward type thing, huh?"

Jenny's blush deepened and her head dipped in embarrassment of this man's astute observation. "As a matter of fact, yes," Jenny said confidently, trying to regain a little composure.

"Good thing I saw you now, instead of then."

"Pardon?" Jenny looked puzzled at him.

"This is not a place for the stuffy, snooty or otherwise. To me it doesn't matter if you come in here wearing bib overalls with a straw hat. You see, I've found through the years that the more fixed-up a person is, the less trustworthy they are. Guess they figure their looks or clothing is gonna impress me. Makes me think they've got somethin' to hide. Whereas, simple attire always takes backseat to personality – it's the person that shines through, not their clothes. I've found them to be the more honest folk. I don't profess to be any psychologist who analyzes all this mumbo jumbo. I just know how I feel. Call me crazy if ya want. Then again, maybe the fact you were plannin' on fixin' up means I should keep my eye on you – that is if you want the job?"

Jenny was speechless.

"Speak up girl. I have difficulty hearing," he said tapping his hearing aide.

"Yes," Jenny blurted, surprised at her quick response. She liked the old man. "By the way, what is your name, Mister. . ."

"Where are my manners. You didn't know you were dealing with a senile old man, did you?"

Jenny smiled.

"My name is Maxwell Saunders. You can call me Max, but don't ever call me any of that mister stuff. Oooh - it makes my blood run sticky."

Jenny giggled. "Okay. But now, back to the job. What about hours?" Jenny said somewhat tensing.

"I'm sure whatever is best for you will be just fine with me. That is of course unless you are looking for full time work?"

"Oh, no-no," said Jenny, "I just want to get out a little. Make some extra spending money."

"Good then, I'll show you around a bit, we'll work out the hours, and that'll be that."

Jenny relaxed. As Max showed her around the bookstore, they carried on a light conversation in between his discussing the variety of books found on the shelves.

"So what brings you out here from the city?" Max inquired.

"My aunt moved out of her house and offered it to me for a while. Since I was between jobs, I decided the change of pace might do me some good. So here I am."

"You said your aunt use to live here? Maybe I know her." Max waited for Jenny's reply.

"Her name is Abbigale Dupree." Jenny had barely said her name when Max interjected ecstatically.

"Abby! What a fine lady. No wonder I liked you from the start. She's a highly valued customer and friend of mine. Good as they come, she is. But you say she moved?"

Jenny saw a puzzled look on Max's face. "Yes, you didn't know?"

"No," Max chimed. "I know she hasn't been in for a while, but she never mentioned anything about moving. Must have been a sudden decision. What I wouldn't give to be able to just up and go like that. Not a care in the world."

Max resumed pointing out some of his rarest books and telling stories about how he had acquired them. Jenny couldn't pinpoint it, yet there was a marked difference in Max's attitude. He didn't ask her any more personal questions, and Jenny didn't pry for any information either. She figured there'd be enough time for all that later.

They concluded their tour of the bookstore. Max decided since he was going out of town for the weekend, it would be best for Jenny to come in on Monday morning. They could work together the first day.

Depending on how things went, he'd start taking some time off and leave her in charge of things. Jenny was pleased with the arrangements. Max shook her hand to seal their agreement. Jenny left the bookstore and headed back to her car.

As she walked down the sidewalk, she mentally re-played her encounter with Max Saunders. Jenny got so caught up in her thoughts she nearly passed right by her car. She reassuringly patted Kit on the hood before hopping into the car. With her hand poised on the key in the ignition, she thought, "Things are definitely looking up. Hardly settled in and already employed. That was the easiest job I ever got, or should I say, *got* me." Jenny turned the key, Kit purred into action. She backed out onto the street and headed back up the hill to the house.

Chapter 11

*A*rriving home, Jenny promptly went into the kitchen and fixed a cup of tea. She had a bit of Max's coffee while touring the store and now her stomach felt like a tar pit. "A cup of raspberry tea will freshen any tired or abused palate." She took her tea into the front room. Jenny sat on the couch and drank her tea slowly, relishing every drop.

The day was getting on. She decided it would probably be best to stay home and unpack a few of the boxes she had brought along from the city. Jenny went through the boxes, pulling some things out and leaving others inside. She didn't really need to have everything unpacked. If she found she couldn't get along without something, she could always retrieve it. When finished sorting through the boxes she put the storable items in what was at one time the maid's quarters, on the main floor just down the hallway from the dining room, back of the staircase.

Now it was time to find homes for the items she had pulled out of the boxes. Most were easy to place in appropriate spots. The knick-knacks were what gave her the most trouble. Jenny found it difficult to fit her cheap relics in with the refined quality already displayed in the house. It took her a lot of mixing and matching, but finally she was satisfied with the results. Now it was beginning to feel a little bit more like home.

Jenny was exhausted. It had been a long day. She was too worn out to eat anything, so she decided to head up to bed. "Maybe I'll read in bed for a while." With that she walked over to the bookshelf by the fireplace and began scanning the shelves for something light to read. "*Poems to Remember*," she said aloud, her eyes fixing on a small leather-bound book. Jenny pulled the book from the shelf and opened to the table of contents. The book was comprised of a variety of interestingly titled poems, along with a wide variety of authors. "This will do nicely." Closing the book, she headed upstairs.

Jenny prepared herself for bed, slipping into a silken nightshirt she had bought last year on a frivolous shopping spree to lift her spirits. Buying something nice and pretty did actually make her feel better. She only wore it when she wanted to make herself feel special. Tonight was no exception, and as always it worked – she felt good. Hopping into bed, she opened the book and started to read. She read about love, life, nature, happiness, sorrow and despair. Her favorite poem was one that made her feel better about herself, like there was reason and purpose for all the things she had gone through in her life. The poem was called "The Lost." The title in the table of contents had intrigued Jenny as to its subject matter. Reading it once wasn't enough. She read it over and over, letting it sink in to somehow reassure her everything *was* okay. "Once more before I turn out the lights," Jenny said, and begun to read the poem for the last time that night.

The Lost
We know that life will always go on,
though times be good or bad.
We've often been told, "Don't give up on yourself,
there's still more fish to be had."
But more times than not, it tears us apart,
to let go of a lover or friend.
Thinking what didn't we do, could there still be a chance?
Not accepting that it's really the end.

Then soon through despair, we hate for the pain,
not thinking of how we have grown.
For each new relationship adds a finishing touch,
that makes a personality our own.
So when the right man comes, wanting you as his wife,
you might stop a moment and pray. . .
Thank God for the lost, for in their own way,
they've helped make you what he loves today.

Jenny closed the book and turned out the light. Somehow, the hurt she had thought was gone from so many past relationships finally was okay. Her bitterness was gone and she could now begin to put to rest the feelings and thoughts of what was past. Jenny turned over on her side to look out the window. As she watched the forest beyond, she felt strange, as though it was watching her. That thought didn't scare her though. Instead, she felt somehow akin. There was a sense of understanding, but of what she didn't know.

Jenny closed her eyes and began to drift off to sleep. Before she knew it, reality had slipped from her awareness. Again, she was journeying into her dreams. Visions of her day and special thoughts of her past drifted by her view as her body began to release its physical tensions. Her body once again gave in to the creation of her inner mind. She drifted slowly, aimlessly, then as if a fog were lifting, the sights and smell of her dream began.

Jenny found herself walking up a grassy hill toward an old deteriorating castle. It had obviously been a central figure at some time in the past. It stood strong. Though the years had tortured its surface, it still boasted much of its fine detailed architecture. Jenny walked up to the front doors. They were tall, dark, and heavy. It would take a battering ram to open these doors, yet, they glided open at the touch of her hand. Jenny felt the wind swirl around her as she gazed toward what had been opened before her. Hesitantly she stepped forward into her dream, far away from reality.

Laying peacefully, bathed in the moon's glow, Jenny looked almost unreal. Her night had just begun. Jenny would not sleep peacefully for long. Her dream would take hold and play with her emotions, until finally before dawn, it would wake her out of fear.

Chapter 12

Jenny woke. A pale morning gray opened her eyes, yet didn't provide the energy to entice movement from her. She lay very still, feeling drained from her dream. She wanted to recall and understand as much of the dream as possible. She knew if she moved too much that the dream would disappear as if it had never happened, leaving only the feelings the dream had evoked to deal with. As patient as she was, the dream eluded her. Finally, with frustration hounding her, she tried to force the dream to come back to her, at which point the dream reared – racing back from whence it came. Having been defeated, she reluctantly pulled herself from the bed. Jenny was not thrilled that she had to deal with emotions stirred by some unknown. Even though it was only a dream, the feelings still felt very real and justified. It would not be easy, but she would have to try to apply some straight logic and disregard – erase – the residue of her dream.

The caffeinated coffee hit the spot. Jenny needed an extra kick this morning. The caffeine gave her the edge she needed to put the night behind her. Breakfast was light. Jenny really didn't have much of a regular appetite. "Today is Saturday. The day the working world lives for. It is the only day that allows no commitments, no schedules, just whimsical plans." Jenny thought about many things to do, but declined, vowing to do them on another day. No, today she would go back into the forest. She needed to go there, especially after last night. Jenny squared things away, then set out for the forest at ten o'clock.

The sky had lightened substantially since Jenny first awoke. Nevertheless, once she stepped into the forest, the sky above became obscured, hiding any sense of light by the thick branches towering above her. Jenny thought she could easily find the place she had visited the other day. She walked very confidently through the forest. Perhaps too confidently. Time passed and she had not found the clearing yet. Her confidence faltered as she realized she had been walking in circles. Feeling adequately frustrated, she sat down on the nearest log.

Jenny was about to give up when she noticed a light spot in the forest ahead. She jumped up and headed straight for it. The closer she got the quicker her stride as she realized she had found the place. Almost running, Jenny quickly halted as she reached the edge of the clearing. It really was as beautiful as she remembered. The gray sky that had haunted the early morning was just a memory now, for the sun shined brightly in the cloudless sky above. The air was warm. A gentle breeze brushed her face as it swirled on its way through the clearing.

This time Jenny walked beyond the rock to the pond. Again, it sparkled enticingly. She removed her socks and shoes, rolled her jeans up and stepped into the water. It was amazingly warm. Was it possible for the pond to be fed by an underground hot spring? Feeling safely isolated, Jenny stepped back out of the water and quickly shed her social skins, then slipped into the pond. The water was so refreshing. She swam and floated quietly, allowing her senses to explore. After a short time, Jenny left the soothing water, dressed, then stretched out on the mossy floor next to the rock. The sun warmed her skin and made her feel quite drowsy. Letting the increasing urge to sleep take charge, Jenny wiggled a bit, nuzzling into a more comfortable position and let go.

Jenny's mind drifted aimlessly. Stress and tension dissipated as her mind continued to wander. She tried to focus her mind on past relationships. She was awfully lonely even with the excitement of this new start on life. It would have been perfect to move to a new place and have the perfect guy just waiting for you. Happiness, love, security, all at one time. Most of the time the solitude in her life was manageable, but basically, Jenny flourished as a person when there was love around her. Maybe it was because her family had been taken from her, never again to hear or touch their love. Surely, a psychologist could come up with a list of reasons, but it didn't change the facts. Jenny needed a deep sense of belonging, affection, and self-fulfillment.

Her mind drifted more vividly now as she began to think about the type of man that was right for her. She honestly wanted to know, not trying to conjure makeovers of men she knew or movie stars she swooned over in the past. As she let her mind try to answer or solve this mystery, she was becoming less aware of the place around her. She began to feel as if her whole body was being lifted from the mossy bed on which she lay. Jenny felt a warm, tingling sensation move through her. Drifting, drifting, separating now from herself in search of someone. She felt as if her mind had shed the body from the restrictions of her physical being. The sensations were unlike any she had felt before. Wondrous, meditative. She began to dream. . .

A sunny day, trees and birds. Jenny was floating above as if akin to the feathered world. Fields of golden grain swayed and moved as water on the open sea – the sun glistening off their feathery tops. A single bird swooped in front of her vision, then another rising from behind, in chase of the first. Jenny watched them. They were flying toward a farm, now visible in the near distance. She too followed the birds, curious as to what lay in store at the farm.

The birds swooped in and out of the barn, spinning, diving, and circling playfully. Jenny, instead, circled the farm slowly. The house, garden, and once around the barn. As she went around the barn, she could hear the clinking of metal, a variety of animals, and then – the low, soft, almost methodic whisper of a man humming. Trying to hear the humming better, she found herself no longer flying but standing outside the barn door. She cautiously peeked inside.

The smell of hay and livestock filled her head. Jenny couldn't see anyone inside the doorway. A stall on her left blocked her view of the rest of the barn. She quietly moved inside. The humming continued, unaware of her presence. Jenny peered around the corner of the stall. There, in the center of the barn, illuminated by a ray of sun from the loft window, was a man that stilled Jenny's heart. He was tall and strong, with hair that shined like the feathers on a Raven's head. Well-tanned from working the land. He was obviously engrossed with the care of what he held in his hand, for his eyes twinkled like pure onyx. He was smiling and humming to the newborn pup wiggling in his gently cupped palm. In a crate just out of the light, Jenny spied the mother dog. She was watching the man with her baby. She seemed rather proud of her accomplishment and the fact that her master was so pleased. As Jenny continued to look, she began to see the rhythmic bopping of other little heads nursing at their mother's belly. The man looked down at his companion and spoke, "Yes, Champion, you should be proud. This is a fine litter you have here." The dog's tongue lapped and tail wagged out of thanks and love for her master.

Jenny was touched by the gentle, kind-hearted interaction between the man and his dog. She felt a warm affection towards this man even though she had only seen him for the first time. Jenny sighed and leaned against the stall, wishing for a similar type of affection. "SNAP!" One of the cross boards on the stall gave way and split apart from under her. "Who's there?" the man jolted in surprise. Jenny gasped. Without thought, she spun around and flew out of the barn, then back up into the air. Feeling safe above, Jenny could hear the man calling and his dog barking. She made one circle of the barn, feeling concealed in the sky. She saw the man and his dog standing outside the barn looking bewildered seeing, their solitude.

Jenny's dream began to fade as she drifted back the direction she had come. What appeared to be a light misty haze began to soften the scenery around her. Gradually, the mist obscured all images within her sight. She no longer felt as if she were flying. Instead, she sensed her mind, her thoughts, floating back to reality. Slowly Jenny became aware of her body as she began to rouse from her sleep. Gently opening her eyes, she felt a slight numbing, tingling sensation beneath her. Jenny rose slightly to see what it was. But as quickly as it faded, she too tired of searching the moss below her.

The sun had descended just below the treetops. Jenny was surprised to see she had spent so much time sleeping. Feeling exhilarated and in a good mood from her dream, Jenny gathered herself up and headed back towards the house.

The walk back seemed to take longer than expected. Jenny walked in the back door at a quarter to four. "Wow," she thought, "I can't believe it's so late. I feel exhausted." She had felt so good earlier, and now, "Well, maybe it's just all that fresh air and the swimming too," she added with increased surety.

All she could think about was bedtime, when she could drop her head into the fluffy bed pillows that awaited her. Her short evening was uneventful as she ate, watched television, then prepared for bed. Even her sleep would be calm – dreamless.

Chapter 13

*S*unday morning came shining through the window, waking Jenny at 6:30 am. She could hear the sounds of what seemed to be a hundred songbirds in the trees outside. It was the start of a beautiful "Indian Summer" type of day. Being her first Sunday in town, Jenny decided to attend service at the local town church. She had seen the church up the hill from the city hall. It would give her an opportunity to meet some of the people in town. Hopefully there would be some nice eligible men as well.

At 8:30am, Jenny left the house. As she drove down the hill, the bells in the church steeple began to chime. A salty breeze came up from the waterfront. The sky was a deep blue except for the few wispy clouds that dotted the horizon.

Jenny reached the church parking lot at a quarter to nine. The townspeople were filing into the building. It seemed to be more of an older crowd than she had hoped for.

The service was good. The preacher – a credit to his profession. Jenny met many in the congregation after the service. She was quite disappointed to see only one or two possible bachelors. Of those possible, not a one appeared to be the least bit interested, or for that fact, worth the bother. Jenny was beginning to realize the expectations she had while still in the city were more suitable for dreams than reality.

The preacher made a point of meeting Jenny. He introduced himself as John Freeman, then proceeded with the normal niceties. Jenny introduced herself as Abbigale's niece, which prompted the preacher to wrestle over a few more of the congregation to meet her. It was obvious Abbigale was well liked in town, but then it wasn't surprising knowing her personality.

A few of the people tried to convince Jenny to stay for their after-service potluck. She begged off giving some excuses about getting ready for her new job the next day.

Jenny went home, changed into some shorts, then ate lunch out on the back porch. Even though it was a nice warm day, Jenny felt rather like a Gloomy-Gus. In an effort to lift her spirits, she tried to convince herself that a life of celibacy was considered a highly redeemable quality by many religious folk. Yet, Jenny couldn't prove the benefits outweighed the detriments of such a lifestyle. Who was she trying to kid? She just couldn't live alone without eventually going crazy. The brutal realization that her character was flawed – not capable of upholding such a devoutly religious lifestyle – plummeted her deeper into a state of self-pity. "No!" she cried. "I'm not going to keep doing this to myself!"

Forcing her thoughts to change track, she began to reminisce about yesterday's journey into the forest. Jenny had felt so good there. Her dreams. . .well, they were intriguing. There was something. . . different. The desire to return began to well up inside her. She looked out at the forest. The tree branches were swaying – or were they actually motioning for her to come back? She felt a tingle of excitement grip her chest. Her breaths changed to short pants of anticipation. "Yeah. . . okay. . . you want me to come, I will!" as she dared to take the challenge.

Mystery, magic, and the unknown were well hidden interests of Jenny's. Now, she was letting these *what ifs* take control. Like living a childhood fantasy, her emotions were allowing her this brief escape from reality. The adrenaline was flowing. Jenny rushed into the house, tossing the remnants of her lunch into the sink. Before the screen door could bounce twice off the frame, she was back out the door heading for that place in the forest.

Chapter 14

Finding the place this time was not difficult at all. In fact, Jenny couldn't understand how she could have had so much trouble the last time. Emerging from the forest into the clearing was like stepping from winter into spring – night into day. It was as beautiful as ever. Jenny immediately headed for the pond. A moment behind the rock and splash, she was again gliding through the refreshing water. As she swam and splashed through the pond, she periodically would see one forest animal or another come into sight. They didn't seem to mind her presence. Birds, rabbits, squirrels, even a few deer roamed through the clearing.

Jenny thought more about her dream from yesterday. She tried to focus on the man. Her curiosity about him was definitely piqued. Maybe another cat-nap might help me remember better, she thought. Deciding it was worth a try, she departed the water in exchange for the soft mossy bed.

Dressed in her clothes, Jenny made herself comfortable next to the rock. The sun's rays again began to warm her like a blanket. She was not as interested in just letting her mind wander like before. Rather, there was a stronger desire to return to the farm she had visited, where the man would surely be. Jenny lay there in the moss, but nothing. She was not dozing off. "I ought to know better. I can't force myself to sleep."

With that, Jenny just relaxed and remembered her frame of mind which preceded the dream yesterday. She allowed something inside her to take control. It was not logic nor raw emotion, but something more understanding, knowing. A part of her she never quite knew how to tap into in the past. Her consciousness was fading. A tingling sensation began to stir from beneath her. In her mind, she could sense a change beginning, from conscious sleep to subconscious awakening. The tingling sensation was making her feel so light, free. She tried to open her eyes. The little amount of focus she could muster only allowed a very narrow blurred vision. All she could see was a haze of white sparkling light. Her eyes gave up, releasing her to dream.

Jenny found herself walking amid swaying waves of golden wheat. She instinctively knew the dirt path beneath her led to the farm. Her pace quickened as she anticipated seeing the man again. Unlike yesterday, today she was more aware of her surroundings. Everything seemed more alive, real. Even her clothes were different. She had on a long, light blue cotton dress, trimmed with white lace and ruffles. Jenny continued down the path, picturing herself as a heroine out of a popular romance novel.

As she neared the edge of the field bordering the farm, she stopped, obscured by the last few shocks of wheat. There was no motion around the house or barn. After a few minutes, feeling rather certain no one was about, Jenny decided to take a look around.

The barn was closest so she walked there first, all the while remembering her last visit. Her heart beat faster as she entered the barn. There was a bit of disappointment as she looked around the corner of the stall and saw no one in sight. As she surveyed the barn, she began to hear a low whimpering sound. She immediately changed her focus to a spot just beyond the sunlight. Slowly, she moved forward. The whimpering seemed to multiply. A smile grew on Jenny's face as she realized what she was hearing. It was the sound of the newborn pups calling for their mother. Jenny kneeled before the box, reaching down to comfort them. One pup tried to climb her arm and instinctively she picked it up cradling it to her chest. The little puppy's nose sniffed inquisitively at her clothes, then stretched up to nibble on her chin. Jenny giggled, as it tickled – the little toothless mouth. She played with the puppies for quite some time, becoming unaware of everything else around her.

Jenny was so preoccupied, she didn't realize she was not alone until the mother, Champion, jumped into the box between Jenny and the puppies. Surprised, she almost fell over backwards but caught herself just in the nick of time. Even though she hadn't fallen on her backside, she now looked like she was ready for a crab-walking race. Jenny felt pretty stupid, but that changed to embarrassment when she heard deep roaring laughter from behind.

Trying to stand up quickly and turn around at the same time, Jenny just managed to twist herself into a knot, finally flipping over face down in the dirt. She considered keeping her face buried there in the dirt as she heard the deep laughter break into a higher hysterical bellowing. Jenny allowed her eyes to look up just as a hand reached down in front of her.

"Excuse me," the deep voice said trying to keep from breaking into more laughter, "let me help you up."

Jenny sheepishly looked up at the man standing before her. His body flinched to keep from bursting out in laughter as he saw this lovely creature's face turn upward looking rather like. . . a creature. . . a raccoon to be exact. Her face was covered with dirt. Luckily for Jenny, this man must have had some pity for her because he just swallowed the laugh, smiled, and tried to look very understanding adding, "Please, take my hand." Jenny took his hand. It was warm and strong as he effortlessly lifted her off the ground.

As Jenny dared to look up into his eyes, a warm rush overtook her. Jenny's knees buckled beneath her. Nearly collapsing, the man braced her arm for a moment until she regained herself.

"My name is Jonathan Windgate," he said with a smile that could very possibly melt a polar ice cap.

Mesmerized by the handsome man before her, Jenny stood speechless. She felt as if his eyes were penetrating straight to her soul. They were like onyx, deep and warm, yet fiery – sparkling with life.

"What's the matter? Cat got your tongue?" he chided as he withdrew a handkerchief from his pocket and handed it to her.

"Oh," her eyes now refocusing, "thank you." She quickly wiped the dirt from her face and hands. "Nice to meet you Jonathan. My name is Jennifer McBride, or Jenny if you like."

"Jenny. . . that's a nice name. . . has a little spunk to it, which, from the looks of things, fits you very well."

Jenny blushed. "I'm sorry for barging in here unannounced. I didn't see anyone around. . . and. . . well. . . these puppies are so cute. . ." she trailed off turning back towards the puppies behind her, not knowing what else to say. She was afraid to look at him for she knew her face was getting redder by the second.

Sensing her uneasiness, Jonathan took her off the hook. "That's quite alright. My home is always open to visitors. But, might I ask, are you from around here? I don't recollect ever seeing you before."

Jenny didn't know what to say. She couldn't tell the truth. He'd never believe her. She could see it now, "This is all just a dream, part of my imagination, I just popped in. . ." he'd be reaching for his shotgun while Champion was off dragging back the men in the white coats. Jenny decided to shoot from the hip, "I don't know. . . exactly."

"What about family?" Jonathan prompted, looking rather concerned.

"There's just me now," she answered sorrowfully.

A troubled look fell over Jonathan's face. "How come you know you haven't any family, yet don't know where you're from?"

"Well," Jenny groped for words, "it's a bit fuzzy. Some things I remember. . . some things I don't."

Jonathan looked puzzled now. Jenny began to worry that her excuse had sounded rather stupid. She was trying to figure another approach when Jonathan blurted out, "Amnesia! That's what it is. You must have hit your head or something." Jenny was thrilled – her excuse had worked. She felt a lot more confident, for now she had an easy way out of any question.

Jonathan, feeling rather proud of his analysis, began hurling questions at Jenny as if he were a junior psychologist, "How far back can you remember? How did you get here?"

Jenny was overwhelmed by the barrage of questions – she needed time to think. "Can we walk outside? I need to get some fresh air. I'm feeling a little weak," Jenny was playing up her part to stall for time.

"Of course, where are my manners. Let's go over to the house. We can sit on the porch out of the sun," he replied, offering his arm to escort her. She obliged, and they walked out of the barn.

As they walked towards the house, Jenny told him what little she could remember, "I found myself in the middle of your field. That's as far back as I know. Kind of like in a dream – you're just there."

"Hmm," he muttered softly. She could see the gears spinning in his head. They walked the rest of the way in silence.

Reaching the house, Jonathan led Jenny up onto the porch, then motioned her to sit on the bench swing.

"Thank you," Jenny said, as she made herself comfortable.

Jonathan disappeared into the house, but shortly returned with a pitcher of lemonade. "Hope this isn't too sour for you. I don't particularly like sweet drinks."

"No. I'm sure it'll be fine. I'm like you with sweets."

He handed a glass of lemonade to Jenny, poured one for himself, then sat down on the porch railing. Jonathan couldn't take his eyes off Jenny.

Intimidated, Jenny started the conversation, "Do you get many visitors out here?"

"No, not many," he answered before taking a long drink of lemonade.

"Is there a town nearby?" Jenny asked.

"There is a town, but it's quite a ways down the road. . ."

This wasn't working. Jenny was getting flustered by his continual and intense stare. It was as if his eyes were an x-ray machine scanning her from head to toe, determining whether she was really made of sugar and spice and everything nice.

Her voice a little unsteady, she asked, "Is there something wrong? Or do you just never blink?" sarcastically emphasizing the word blink.

"Oh, I'm sorry. I wasn't aware I was staring. You must think me awfully rude. It's just, you are a very beautiful woman," he finished with a warm sincere expression on his face.

Jenny's breaths grew short for a moment as she realized there was definitely a mutual attraction between the two of them. "As long as you guarantee you're not an axe murderer or anything of the sort, then I'm flattered." Jenny stared back deep into his eyes. He smiled.

Jenny and Jonathan sat talking on the porch while the sun crossed over the front of the house. She managed to keep the conversation focused mainly on Jonathan. She did however, throw in thoughts and opinions, and any feelings she could discuss without getting too detailed. Jonathan even sported a few jokes that had Jenny holding her sides with laughter. It all seemed so natural. It was as if they had been friends for years.

"Jenny, I really like your company. We could probably talk all night and not realize the time. We need to figure out what we're going to do with you before the sun disappears over the horizon."

"Oh, I guess you're right," Jenny replied not sounding very enthusiastic. Jonathan picked up on her reluctance. "Now. . . I know this may not sound proper. . . but. . ."

The proverbial butterfly began to ricochet inside of Jenny.

". . . if you'd like. . . I'd really enjoy having you stay for supper."

Jenny's eyes lit up. "Yes, I'd like that a lot."

"Then," Jonathan continued looking a little unsure of himself," I have a spare room – it would be too late to go into town – just for the night, I assure you. I'd take you to town in the morning. See if we can figure out who you are."

Jenny was thrilled, though she knew better than to show her excitement. "That's very generous of you," she began, immediately wanting to curl up in a corner as she realized her voice sounded like some snooty, "prim and proper" old maid. She was obviously overcompensating *way* too much! She attempted to soften her response, "I suppose it would be a lot wiser to head for town in the morning. I think I've come to know you well enough today to trust you. At least for one night."

Jonathan grinned. "Great! Now since that is all settled shall we adjourn inside," he said as he gestured like a butler ushering in dinner guests.

Jonathan obviously found great humor in her response. Realizing her awkwardness, he pretended to play along with the mood she'd set. How sweet of him to have not taken offense. So Jenny continued, this time enjoying the charade, "Oh, by all means, let's do adjourn!" retorting as if she had been instantly transformed into a royal stuffed shirt, or – should she say – dress. She giggled as she sashayed through the doorway.

Jonathan humored by her quick response to continue the playacting followed with, "I hope my lady won't be too terribly disappointed with the modest meal and humble entertainment."

"Oh my. . . entertainment you say?" Jenny ribbed him, "Now this could be interesting."

"Well. . . I hope I'm not too dull of a host" he quickly responded.

"I don't see how anyone could ever think you dull," Jenny boldly pumped his ego, while staring straight into his eyes.

There was so much electricity flying between them, one would think a horrendous storm was brewing. Jenny was tingling all over. She hadn't felt this good in years. Actually, she couldn't remember a time she had felt so content and relaxed, yet immensely excited.

Jonathan went into the kitchen, Jenny tailgating. She tried to help him with the meal but he wouldn't have it. He'd throw in comments like, "Guests don't cook," "The kitchen's too small," or her favorite, "Please, I'm trying to impress you with my culinary skills." That was the clincher. Jenny resolved herself to merely talking and watching.

It seemed they had only started a minute ago when Jonathan announced dinner was ready. They sat down at the table. Jonathan served them both. "Cornbread, chili, and a fresh green salad," he boasted.

"I haven't had chili in ages. From the look and smell of it, you cook one mean pot of chili. But," Jenny added, "someone would think you were already expecting company by the size of this pot."

Jonathan looked a little sheepish but insisted he liked chili a lot. "I could eat it for breakfast, lunch and dinner. Besides," he said in a more muffled tone," it happens to be the only edible thing I can cook!" Then, with a smirk he continued," Throw a little sour cream on top and *ta-da*, we have dessert!"

"Seriously?" Jenny said as they both laughed.

Jonathan and Jenny continued eating their dinner while talking about a mish-mash of things – trivia, life, likes and dislikes. Their conversation seemed endless, both had a million things they wanted to say and share with each other. Every new subject spurred new thoughts and ideas in each other. Only as the last dinner dish was dried did either take notice how pitch black it had become outside.

"Gosh," Jenny said, "we must have been talking for hours!"

"I'll say! But then, how does the saying go? 'Time flies when you're having fun.'" They had been so completely engrossed in each other's company they wouldn't have noticed even if a tornado passed outside, unless it had landed directly on the house!

Jonathan offered Jenny an after dinner drink. "We can sit out on the porch swing and enjoy a little of the night sky and maybe even see a few shooting stars." "Sounds like a wonderful idea," Jenny answered. She was happy to know Jonathan wasn't ready to end their evening either.

They went out to the porch. A soft warm breeze made its way across the covered porch. Jenny stopped, turned into the breeze and closed her eyes. She wanted to feel the breeze caress her skin as it drifted lazily around her.

Opening her eyes Jenny caught Jonathan watching her intently from the porch swing. In that same moment, Jonathan, suddenly realizing Jenny was aware of his staring, quickly picked up his drink and took a sip.

Jenny moved over to the porch swing and sat down next to him. They gently swung back and forth, silently, sipping their drinks. It wasn't an awkward silence. Both were relishing the newness of this rapidly growing attraction they shared for each other. Their minds busily recalling the other's words and feelings that were openly shared, trying to permanently imprint them in their minds. Neither wanted to forget a single word. They continued to swing, watching the stars and feeling the closeness of each other. Both their faces reflecting a smile of happiness and contentment.

Jenny indulged herself further by laying her head back and closing her eyes. Resting her head on the swing's back made her even more relaxed. She was in Seventh Heaven. She closed her eyes for a moment hoping to envision what their future together would be like. Jenny's wishful thoughts were unwantingly interrupted by what sounded like faint but increasingly louder whispering. Jenny was so carried away in her thoughts, she hadn't heard what Jonathan had said.

"I'm sorry, what did you say?" Jenny apologized, opening her eyes and turning toward Jonathan.

He was gone, and so was Jenny. Gone from Jonathan's porch – back in the forest again. She wept quietly remembering it had only been a dream.

Chapter 15

*J*enny returned to the house just as the sun slipped behind the trees. She had walked back home not allowing her mind to linger on any one thought. She just didn't feel like thinking about anything, so she concentrated on nothing. Even though it was dinnertime, Jenny wasn't hungry. Her stomach actually felt quite satisfied. Her first day of work started tomorrow. She decided to turn in early as to be fresh and alert come morning.

Jenny shivered. For some reason she felt rather cold and achy. "A nice hot bath might just do the trick," she told herself hoping silently she wasn't coming down with a cold. She soaked in the tub for a good hour. By the time she had finished, the aches and cold had faded away. Jenny got into bed at 7:30 p.m.

Reading for half an hour, Jenny tried to make herself sleepy. It wasn't difficult. Even with the long sleep she had in the forest. Her eyes began to close with the weight of sleep. She fought the heaviness only to finish a paragraph. Once done, Jenny closed the book laying it down on the nightstand, and turned off the light.

Jenny lay gazing out the window toward the forest. She pulled the covers up around her neck in attempt to ward off the cold she sensed from beyond the window's edge. Slowly her eyes closed as she drifted off to sleep.

Jenny found herself in the white flowing gown atop a hill covered with long swaying grass. The wind swirled the grass like beaters on a mixer. Left, then right, circling new designs every second. She was not cold, yet the sky was slate gray – cold and dark. The wind began to circle around her now. Lightly, then more forcibly until she began to feel like Dorothy from the *Wizard of Oz*, caught in the middle of a tornado. It pushed and pulled, slapping her hair like a thousand whips across her face. Frantically she fought to keep her balance. The wind shoved her relentlessly, moving her toward the decaying castle. Only this time the castle seemed more like a refuge away from the wind.

The castle doors flew open as if they were made of paper. The wind cast Jenny on her knees just inside the door. With tears in her eyes, Jenny pushed the tangled hair out of her face. She turned her head up toward the vicious wind outside, expecting to see the shape of some evil entity lurking within it, but there was nothing. It was just a mild breeze blowing beyond the castle walls.

Bewildered, Jenny got up to her feet and began to silently wander into the belly of the castle. Aimlessly, almost trance-like, she seemed to float from room to room. She was looking for something, but she wasn't sure what it was. Jenny felt as though each room belonged to different people. No, that wasn't quite it. It was more like entering the thoughts and dreams of many different minds. Each from faraway lands and times. Jenny kept moving, not knowing what to make of it all. She continued to search but as she left each room, she felt some-how weaker than in the last. A cold sliver of fear pierced her heart as she realized she might not find it in time. "So many rooms, and so little time!" she muttered exhaustedly. Room, after room, after room. They began to swirl around her – a never-ending maze on a never stopping carousel.

7:00 a.m., the alarm clock sounded. Jenny sat up in bed with a start. It was Monday morning. Her first day of work. Jenny didn't feel as rested as she'd hoped to. "Ugh. . . couldn't I have just one more hour of sleep? Please?" she asked herself, then looked at the alarm clock wishing it really said six instead of seven. When the clock failed to magically change, Jenny relented and dragged herself out of bed. She shuffled down to the bathroom.

Flipping on the light, she looked in the mirror. "Eeee-gads! It's Fright Night III! Bring out the garlic! The Crucifixes! And open those darn shades so the sun can chase this creature back where it came from!" With her fingers crossed like a crucifix, Jenny pretended to sizzle a mark on her forehead. "I don't understand how the soap opera stars do it. They look better waking up then I do leaving the house. Like they're permanently pressed. . . having that air-brushed ambiance (she mockingly posed) . . . or should I say air-*head* ambiance!" Jenny giggled at herself. "Why, you're just a regular side-buster, Jenny McBride!"

Jenny brushed her teeth then hopped in the shower – piping hot, she liked it! Guaranteed to take all the kinks out of you, if it didn't melt you first.

By 7:30am Jenny was dressed and heading downstairs for break-fast. There was a definite spring in Jenny's step. She was looking for-ward to her first day of work. Being a book-lover herself, it wouldn't be difficult for Jenny to pass away any slow streaks during the day. This was the perfect type of job for her.

"Breakfast is going to be big today," Jenny announced to the kitchen. "I'm famished!" She began pulling out the food. Eggs, bacon, onions, cheese, green salsa, tomatoes, hash browns – well actually Tator Tots, which she would smash into hash browns in the frying pan – bread, and some butter. As she was pulling the food out, anticipation of the end result was too much for her stomach. It let out one of the most demand-ing and inpatient grumbles she had ever heard. "Hungry are we?" she chided, looking down at her belly. She was immediately answered by a variety of little grumbles.

Jenny fired up the stove, put on some water, and began cooking. In no time, her breakfast was ready. Crisp bacon, oven baked toast, hash browns, and an absolutely delicious omelet. Upon making her cup of tea, Jenny sat down to eat. She ate slowly, wanting to savor every bite. After finishing her meal, Jenny washed her dishes, finishing up right at half past eight.

Jenny wanted to arrive at the bookstore before nine o'clock, to show Mr. Saunders that she was better than punctual. She couldn't remember exactly how long it took to drive there since she wasn't really concerned about watching the clock the first time she drove through town.

A couple butterflies began to stir inside her. She took a deep breath, "Time to get cracking." Jenny made sure everything was off, then grabbed her purse and coat. She flew outside closing the door behind her. Kit was at the curb waiting anxiously. She was sure Kit was waiting by the way he started right up. Jenny swung the car around and headed down the hill toward town.

Chapter 16

*M*r. Saunders was just pulling up the shades when Jenny drove up. She smiled and waved at him, and he returned to her a crusty two-finger salute off the brim of his cap.

Jenny got out of her car as Mr. Saunders fumbled a little with the front door lock. She waited at the door patiently, then he opened the door for her and she walked in as the overhead bell still echoed from the door. "Good Morning, Mr. Saunders".

"Max – call me Max," he chided. "I'm anything but formal," he professed stubbornly.

"I'm sorry *Max* – my mistake."

"Let's see that it doesn't happen again!" Max remarked, pretending he was a snobby old school teacher or such.

"Oh yes, mister. . . Max!" Jenny responded boldly.

Max just frowned at her muttering, "Impossible, hard-headed kids." Jenny laughed.

Max spent the morning going over procedures, forms, and a variety of miscellaneous - but important and pertinent – information. This was all broken up with several coffee breaks. Max made it very clear that he was not running a store so he could run himself into the ground. As he put it, "Part of job satisfaction is job enjoyment. And sittin' drinkin' a cup of coffee is pure enjoyment to me!"

Max had Jenny fill out the necessary employment paperwork while he sat at his desk pretending to be gazing out the window, when he was really trying to sneak in 10 to 20 winks. The rest of the morning was spent just familiarizing herself.

Jenny was engrossed with reading book titles when Max yelled over.

"Jenny?"

"Yes, Max?"

"You like cheeseburgers?"

"I love them!"

"Good, cuz I took the liberty of ordering a couple for us from the Surfside. And since I'm buyin', you're flyin'."

"No problemo," Jenny quickly responded.

Max gave her the money and off she went. Only the video and antique store stood between them and the Surfside. Granted, the bar & grill was at the opposite side of the Surfside, but it did have an outside window for take-out orders.

Jenny was back to the bookstore within ten minutes. Max and Jenny sat at the desk by the window devouring their burgers. Both ate as if they hadn't eaten for weeks. They talked mainly about books. Max had the most interesting experience, being that he was into rare and hard to find titles. Not only did the books he described sound interesting, but also the hoops, loops, and obstacles he encountered trying to obtain the books. Max was a very entertaining character. Jenny was glued to his every word.

After lunch, Max had Jenny finish looking over the books. "Take your time," he said, "there's no rush. I'd rather you go slow to see them all, than fast and not remember a one".

A few people came in to browse. Max always approached them first for help, so as not to let them embarrass Jenny by her inexperience. Jenny was very relaxed for her first day. The job was so low key and Max was great. He didn't push her one bit. He said he would rather her jump forward when she was ready.

By the end of the day, Jenny was feeling pretty comfortable with the books. She even had Max quiz her a couple of times.

"Jenny?" Max called.

"Yes, Max?"

"It's four o'clock. I'd like to go over a few things with you for tomorrow, and then I'll show you how I close up."

"Okay, Max," Jenny answered replacing a book back in its place on the shelf.

"Tomorrow," Max began, "I'd like you to concentrate on customer files. This bookstore being the type it is, you'd be surprised at the radius from where the clientele comes. I also do a lot of telephone sales as my store is listed with many other regular bookstores and libraries in the region."

Jenny raised her eyebrows in surprise. "Wow – I didn't realize. But I guess after looking at some of the books, I shouldn't be surprised. That sounds great, Max."

"Also Jenny, since you're training right now, there's no need for you to be in so early, and I'm sure you still have some settling in to do as well."

Jenny nodded. "I guess you're right. I've really only had one look around town, and haven't even gone into all the rooms in the house yet."

"Alright then," Max decided, "why don't you come in around noon and you can work till four. That ought to give you plenty of time to learn everything, and still leave you time to adjust to your new home."

"Terrific," Jenny said with a sigh. "I really appreciate it."

"No problemo," Max replied, mimicking her response at lunch. "Come next week we can decide on a regular work schedule. I need a few days myself to do a little thinking and planning – for my free time that is." Max looked like a kid anticipating summer vacation. "Now that we've got that settled. Let me show you the things you need to do to close the store."

"Okay," said Jenny as she followed Max over to the cash register.

By five o'clock, they were finished. All that was needed to be done, was done. All that was needed to be said, was said.

"Goodnight, Max."

"See you tomorrow," he said as he locked the door behind her. As she drove off, Max was pulling down the last shade.

Even though it had been an easy day, Jenny was still a bit exhausted. Tension can wear a person down fast, regardless of the physical exertion.

In celebration of her first day of work, Jenny stopped by the grocery store and picked up a pizza. As she drove uphill toward home, she couldn't help but imagine the bubbling thick cheese, the smell of sizzling pepperoni. Her mouth began to water in anticipation and her foot instinctively pressed harder on the gas pedal.

It was a beautiful evening. The sun was still shining bright enough when Jenny got home, that she decided to eat her pizza out on the front porch. While the pizza was cooking, Jenny popped open a bottle of wine, grabbed a glass from the cupboard and went out on the porch. There was little to no breeze, so the porch was rather toasty, being in direct sunlight virtually all day. After pouring a glass of wine Jenny sat back in the porch swing, sipped her wine, and passively thought how Jonathan's presence was the only lacking thing to make her evening perfectly complete.

The only cognizant movement by her came when the buzzer on the oven sounded. "Dinner is served," Jenny said as the bounced to her feet, her stomach grumbling all the way to the kitchen. She put the whole pizza, less one slice, on a large cutting board and carried it out to the porch with the one extra piece rapidly disappearing into her now chipmunk-cheeked mouth.

The distant sound of the surf and a few chirping birds kept her musically mesmerized for a good hour while she finished her dinner. Jenny was warm, cozy, full, and just all around feeling good!

As the sun set, the air began to cool. The day had been great, but a long one at that. Her full stomach zapped what little energy see had left. Jenny took her dinner dishes inside. After finishing the dishes, she slowly dragged herself upstairs to the bathroom. There, she ran the water in the tub. First, a nice relaxing hot bath, then to bed, she promised herself.

Jenny soaked for a good half-hour before reluctantly pulling herself from the tub. By the time her head hit the pillow, Jenny was well on her way to sleep. "Everything's going to be okay," she thought to herself, as she turned toward the window – her eyes now fixed on what lay beyond.

Inevitably, her eyelids fluttered, first quickly, then slower as the weight of sleep became too heavy. As Jenny lay still, her features softened – appearing more youthful with the onset of sleep.

All was quiet and peaceful. Outside a gentle breeze played with the plants and trees, only tickling the grass now and then.

Jenny remained motionless for most of the night except when the breeze would shift into high, gusting a sound that seemed to whisper, "Jenny. . . Jen-n-y-y-y."

Chapter 17

For the next few days, Jenny made good use of her mornings off. Tuesday was laundry and cleaning, with a little television in between. Wednesday she went to check out the apparel store and see if their styles were today's or from twenty years ago. Having burned off several calories trying on clothes, she stopped into the ice cream store before going next door to the catalog store to pick up one of their catalogs. She had just enough time before work to set up new patient records at the medical/dental offices.

Thursday, Jenny made herself more familiar with all the rooms in the house. Opening doors and drawers, looking over shelves and anything else that seemed of interest. The last door she opened in the hall surprised her. She had expected another closet of some sort, instead she found a narrow staircase leading up.

Jenny excitedly climbed the stairs, two at a time. At the top. . . another door. She turned the knob but nothing happened. Stopping for only a moment, she tried again, but this time she leaned into it and pushed.

The door gave way and squeaked on its hinges in old discomfort. Beyond the door she found a musty, dim lit attic cluttered with dusty old trunks and forgotten furnishings.

As antsy as a kid in a candy store, Jenny envisioning her finds, she began to sift through the relics from years past. The rest of Thursday morning and most of Friday morning were spent in that candy store of family treasures acquainting herself with the styles and characteristics of relatives before her time. Now, the previously black and white pictures in the family photo albums began to take on a different hue, becoming more colorful as she sifted deeper through the trinkets and personal items of each family member.

Conveniently, a tall slender mirror stood in the corner of the attic through which Jenny could hold up old dresses and pretend she was back in time, adorned with all the frills of that era. The attic was obviously a place where Jenny would choose to spend some of her free hours.

The days went by fast. The mornings she spent familiarizing herself with the house and the surrounding town, then with work in the afternoons.

Jenny found it exciting to walk the aisles of books, reading the titles, stopping at some to take a quick glance inside. Books were not the only things she found interesting. Mr. Saunders, Max, had account files on many of the people in town. Jenny felt she had a better insight into the true personalities of the townspeople by seeing the types of books they would request. And the phone-in files – it was amazing the radius at which Max's books were in demand. His accounts were not only local and national, but Max even had several international accounts! Ooh-la-la! Jenny really enjoyed Max. He began to take on the role of a father/grandfather figure. Max had never had any kids and maybe that emptiness is what helped make him take such a strong shining to Jenny.

The first week passed quickly. Jenny had learned a lot, and her confidence showed. Max would ask her questions for practice, and by Friday, she was able to quickly answer them all. He was pleased with the progress she had made. Only a week and he felt quite comfortable leaving the store in Jenny's capable hands.

By late afternoon on Friday, Jenny was running the store by herself. Max was there, but with his feet kicked up on his desk by the window. He had told Jenny he would be working on a schedule, but several times she glanced back to see Max snoring with a pad of paper lying on his chest. By the end of the day, and week, Jenny was ready for the weekend.

On her way home, as Kit's gears churned, so did the gears in her head as she thought about all the possible things she might do over the weekend.

As Jenny drove up the hill, the trees in the forest seemed to beckon her home. Just for a moment, her mind slipped into neutral as a memory of the place drifted through her mind, body and soul, like some angelic spirit.

Reaching home, Jenny stood – arms folded on Kit's roof – and quizzically surveyed the house and forest beyond. Jenny tried to envision Aunt Abbigale as a young woman, and imagined she was looking at the house on a day, years past, when it was filled with people busying around about nothing. Then, the thought was broken by the sound of a dog yapping noisily down the road.

Jenny headed up to the house. The porch looked inviting – warmed again by the late afternoon sun. Her mind flit to the attic, picturing Abby in some of the beautiful old-fashioned dresses she had found in the attic trunks.

An idea popped into Jenny's head – to play dress up, pretending she was back in time. She hurried into the house, dropped her purse and keys, then ran up to the attic gathering a few of the prettiest dresses she had seen. Carefully she walked back down to her bedroom, arms overflowing with yards of lace and frills.

Jenny felt like a little girl. Before trying on the clothes, she opened the windows and turned on her radio. "Some soft classical music should do it. The type that makes you think of sipping champagne in a bath of scented oils, surrounded by an array of fragrant flowers and candles. . . Hmm, candles in daylight add warmth to any room, lifting any spirit with a glow of happiness." Jenny had found a hurricane lamp in one of the hall cabinets a few days ago. She quickly retrieved it, set it on the dresser, and then proceeded to light it.

"Now, for the fun," Jenny began humming along to the radio's familiar tune as she stepped into the first dress. Looking at herself in the mirror, she felt like Cinderella. She swayed slightly from side to side in sync with the music. Not leaving the width of the mirror, she watched as the folds of lace flowed gracefully in harmony with her body. When the song on the radio stopped, Jenny slipped out of the dress and gently laid it on the bed. Feeling rather parched, she grabbed her robe and headed for the kitchen, dancing a semi-timid waltz down the hallway, twirling once at the head of the stairs before descending.

In the kitchen, Jenny cut up some cheese, washed a stem of grapes, and pulled out a chilled bottle of White Zinfandel. She pulled a tray down from off the top of the fridge and placed the food and wine decoratively across the tray. She grabbed a few napkins from the holder on the kitchen table. Turning back around to the tray on the sink counter, she glanced out the window and her eye caught what seemed to be movement just beyond the edge of the forest. Jenny stopped. Staring hard now, she couldn't find anything, though she felt very sure about having seen something. Oh well, she thought, shirking the idea and moving on to the tray. She sprightly picked up the tray and headed back upstairs, humming the tune she could faintly hear on the radio.

Back in her room, she continued trying on the beautiful dresses, dancing around the room, stopping only briefly to sip her wine or nibble on some food. Jenny tried to picture her relatives dressed in the various dresses. It was a bit hard for her to picture their faces, so instead she began to conjure a scenario of her Aunt Abbigale floating beautifully around the backyard at her eighteenth birthday party, when she first met Aaron von Dorne. How beautiful he must have envisioned her.

Jenny went to the window half expecting to see the party in full swing below. As she stood looking out the window, a warm breeze carrying a faint seashore scent flowed through the window, circling the room in a cleansing sweep. She breathed deeply. A bright and lively medley began to play stirring Jenny to turn up the volume and make haste for the backyard, as if her presence would solidify the reality of the party.

Wineglass in hand, Jenny pretended to toast with many different guests. She swirled and twirled to the music. It was exhilarating! She began to spin, spin, spin. Her heart was light and full of joy. She began to remember her dream with Jonathan. Spin, spin. The party lights at the far end of the yard flickered brightly. She was in heaven.

"Wait!" Jenny shouted, stopping abruptly, facing the back of the house. Frozen, almost afraid to move, she ever so softly warned herself, "This isn't real, there aren't any party lights anywhere." She momentarily caught a glimpse of a flicker or two in the reflection of the kitchen window. It made the light appear to be closer to the forest.

A 180 off her heel and she was facing the now slowly dimming forest edge. No lights. No flickering. No anything. "Wow, this is spooky," she said uneasily and finished with the famous musical intro to *Twilight Zone*. "What is it? Or should I say what was it? It'd be one thing if it had happened only once. But this is twice, even three times. . . in one day yet! Funny, I don't really feel that unnerved by it. Maybe I've watched too many movies where *strange* is becoming second nature."

Jenny stood for a while watching the forest. After a few minutes had passed, even though Jenny wasn't really afraid of the strange sight she had seen, her desire to stay outside, exposed, was quickly dwindling. She went back inside.

Back in her room, Jenny stepped out of the frilly dress and slipped into her robe. Her train of thought had definitely changed tracks. She carried the dresses back up to the attic, placing them carefully back into the trunks they had come from. Her thoughts volleyed between analyzing the lights and Mrs. Baxtor's last sight of Abbigale walking into the forest. . . the lights, Abbigale, and somewhat intermittently – Jonathan's smiling face. The music seemed more of an interference to her now. Turning the radio off and blowing out the candle, she carried the tray back to the kitchen, silently, in deep thought.

Finally, back in her room Jenny jumped up on the bed, landing with her head deep between the pillows. She rolled onto her side, putting a tight cuddle lock on Teddy. Gazing out the opened window, the forest began to look like a protecting line of sentries. Her mind narrowed its focus down to one single thought – Jonathan, and the place where she first dreamt of him, deep in the forest. "Tomorrow," Jenny whispered, "I'll go back there tomorrow."

Chapter 18

Pitter-patter, pitter-patter
Saturday morning starts with chatter
Pitter-patter, pitter-patter
Rain can make your heart grow sadder

The sound of raindrops roused Jenny from her sleep. A sigh of disappointment escaped her lips as she realized the day would be gloomy if the rain kept up. She felt a chill pass over her as she realized she had fallen asleep on top of her bed. The bedspread, which she must have pulled over her sometime in the night, barely took the cool breeze from the open window off her legs. She would rather have been toasty underneath the sheets and blankets.

Jenny turned on the radio. The weather report was up next. She timed it just right. After a local advertisement had finished, the weatherman began his forecast.

"Don't let today's rain change your plans. This light precipitation is expected to move on within the hour. The clouds will break and the sun will warm us up to a pleasant 72 degrees. Sunday should follow with early morning low clouds, then breaking by late morning, again giving us a mild day. . ." He continued with weather in other parts of the state and country – Jenny wasn't interested. She turned the station to the oldies, which had just started playing, *Leader of the Pack*.

Jenny hopped out of bed and pulled her heavy full-length robe out of the closet, and quickly bundled up in it as she stepped into her slippers. While the music played, Jenny took a long hot shower. She had to take the chill off her bones somehow, or she'd never get warm no matter what the temperature got up to. By the time she had finished her shower and was back in her room, the rain had stopped and the clouds were already thinning. Yes, blue sky was on its way. It was definitely going to be a nice day.

After dressing, Jenny went downstairs for breakfast. In the mood for something light and healthy, it was no time before she had finished. She sat at the table a while longer sipping her coffee slowly while gazing out the kitchen window. The forest beyond seemed to beckon her outside with the enthusiasm of a child wanting to play. She began to think about the place, her daydreams, and Jonathan. Enthusiasm began to stir in her as well, enough to spring her from her chair and prepare to go into the forest.

A few things were needed before she could leave. A blanket, munchies, soda, towel (in case she swam in the pond), drawing materials, an old transistor radio from the kitchen -- anything that she might want while she was there. "Better prepared than lacking," she always told herself. She put everything in an oversized beach bag. Jenny threw her jacket on, then out the door she went.

The air outside was fresh and surprisingly warm. As she walked through the back yard, she saw Mrs. Baxtor looking out her window in Jenny's direction. Jenny thought about acting as if she hadn't seen her, but changed her mind, then smiled and waved at her. Even from that distance, Jenny saw a smile come to Mrs. Baxtor's face, and she returned the wave, raising her hand timidly behind the glass. Jenny felt good as she crossed over into the edge of the forest. Her step was quick in anticipation of the time she envisioned having.

In no time she found herself passing the last trees that etched the place she had become so fond of. As she stepped out into the open, the sunlight bathed her in a blanket of warmth. She turned her face up towards the sun and let the rays penetrate their heat as her mouth opened with an "ahhhhhh. . ." of sheer pleasure. "This is wonderful," she said returning her gaze forward.

Just as Jenny took a step, she heard a rustling of branches. Glancing right, she saw the pink padded feet of a white rabbit as they disappeared under a bush. The rabbit's retreat into the bush flushed two small birds from their resting-place. They shot into the air, chirping wildly, circling up, then spiraling down, whipping around twice above her head – finally flying off to a higher perch in one of the bordering trees.

Jenny walked over to the rock. The moss looked greener and plusher than the last time she had been here. She set down her bag and began unloading her things. Having finished, she turned on her radio, grabbed her towel and headed to the water for a swim. Jenny swam for nearly an hour floating through the water as a collection of harp and flute music played soothingly through the air. After her swim she dried off, dressed, ate, then chose to sketch some of her surroundings. After some time of blending her charcoals to her satisfaction, Jenny put the drawing pad down, yawning. She began to think about Jonathan. She lay down atop the soft moss, it felt like velvet, caressing her body, removing any tension left within her. Covered with the sun's warmth, Jenny quickly dozed off with only Jonathan's name lingering on her lips.

Chapter 19

The sound of puppies yipping, calling for their mother's milk, pressed Jenny's mind to consciousness. She was in the barn, Jonathan's barn. In front of her were the Champion's new pups. But where was Champion? She heard some distant, anxious barking, and assumed Champion must be outside chasing butterflies or something. She disregarded it. "Oh, you poor babies, is your mother neglecting you?" she said, petting each puppy. One of the puppies was trying to crawl up her arm. She gave in and picked him up. Jenny rubbed noses with the puppy. He decided she was the next best thing to his mother and began trying to suckle her nose. Jenny laughed. The toothless mouth tickled. She was so engrossed with the pup she didn't see Champion until she jumped in with her brood. Champion laid down but kept deliberate eye contact with Jenny until she returned the pup.

"So there you are," came a voice from behind Jenny. It was Jonathan. "I was wondering where you had taken off to."

Jenny could feel her face get warm, she just hoped she wasn't too noticeably flushed. "Oh, I didn't realize you were looking for me," Jenny replied. Unlike most dreams, she realized the gap between the last time she saw him and now, but he didn't seem to notice. "I've been watching the puppies."

"They are pretty irresistible aren't they?" Jonathan said as he sat down next to her.

They sat, cooing at the pups, stroking their silky black coats. It was obvious that Champion was full of pride for her pups. Every so often Jonathan would pet Champion's head, she'd respond by raising her head just so, and licking the air in front of her, letting her gaze turn up to Jonathan.

As Jonathan continued petting the puppies, his eyes lowered, seeming distant, and unsure. "I've been thinking," he said.

"Oh, about what?" her eyes searching his face for any indication of what he was thinking.

"I think we should ride into town and see if anyone has any idea about your identity. We could start at the Sheriff's office, then some of the shops. If we don't have any luck there, then we could put a notice in the paper and. . ."

"No!" Jenny interrupted. Jonathan was taken back. His eyes turned inquisitively toward her. Seeing this, Jenny quickly began stuttering nonsensically ". . . well. . . I. . . um. . ." which quickly got a raised eyebrow from Jonathan.

Jenny sighed, "I mean, I'm not ready to go anywhere until I feel a little more *sure* of things. I want to try to remember more. What if the people I came from were horribly rough on me? Would I want to stand out there and say, "Who do I belong with?" Don't you see, anyone could say I belonged to them and I wouldn't know the better." Jonathan looked as though he was carefully considering what Jenny had said, evaluating the probable situations. He nodded his head in agreement. "You may have a point there.

"But," he said looking strongly into her eyes, "what do you suggest we do?"

Jenny, having succeeded in buying time to come up with a past to suit him, was now on the spot. Her heart spoke before her intellect could respond. Trying to avert his melting eyes that held her fast, she could feel the faint warmth of blush rising on her cheeks. "I thought maybe, if you didn't mind. . ." a small smile started to curve at the corner of Jonathan's mouth as he anticipated her response. ". . . I could remain here for a while. Maybe I can begin remembering some things. I would feel so much more comfortable and secure. . . I mean being I've already met and know you. I. . . I don't know anyone else and I'm very leery to trust anything or anyone at this point, and. . ."

"Okay! Okay already!" Jonathan cut her off chuckling. "How flattered I feel," he said so gallantly. "But, are you so sure you can trust me?" His smile was so uplifting, and those eyes. . . his eyes seemed to burn right through to her very soul. She wasn't sure what to make of his response. The thought never crossed her mind that he was anything but a true-blue type of guy, yet. . . his eyes. The air about him began to make her wonder if he *didn't* want to be trusted. Or maybe it was her own feelings awakening inside that colored her perception.

Jonathan had expected a smug response from Jenny, but instead, he was surprised to see her draw back. Somehow, she looked different just then. Not afraid, yet she wouldn't meet his eyes. Suddenly Jonathan felt as if he'd made a big mistake with what he'd said. Maybe now she might *want* to leave. He couldn't let that happen. In just the short time he'd known her, she had begun to fill the elusive emptiness within him. That part of him nothing even came close to touching. He now realized the question he asked wasn't a question of whether he could be trusted, she could trust him with her life, but rather that he didn't want to be limited or obligated to keeping any distance from her. He wanted her to stay. He wanted to know everything about her. He wanted *her*.

Quickly Jonathan retracted jokingly, "I'm sorry, I shouldn't have made a joke like that with all you've been through. Yes, of course you are safe here," and with a longing deep inside, "you may stay as long as you wish." The gentleness with which he spoke made Jenny raise her eyes to meet his. His eyes were aglow with a warmth and strength that made Jenny smile brightly, feeling safe.

Time must have frozen for just a moment, for neither realized their lack of words. They were both fixed – eyes reading eyes, sensing something new beginning. Then a cool breeze swept around them, ebbing the rising currents that held them.

Champion barked. Both turned. "Not getting enough attention, Champ, huh?" Jonathan kidded. Champion seeming to comprehend him, gave a half-bark in response, then lowered her attention back to her pups, licking their coats and mothering the squirming brood.

"Well, I'm glad we've got that all settled. Why don't we leave Champion with her pups for now and go to the house for something to quench our thirst."

"It is rather warm," Jenny said, though she inwardly wasn't at all referring to the weather.

They left the barn and Champion behind them. Walking toward the house, Jenny realized things were changing between them. She was afraid. She was excited. She was uncertain about herself and where they were headed.

As the days passed, Jonathan brought a new sense of belonging to Jenny. Something she'd never felt before. He made her laugh. Her emotions found new heights of love, caring, and adoration. She could sit and listen to him talk for hours, completely mesmerized. Hungrily, soaking in every word he said, awakening a new wonder, an excited anticipation of life. Never before had she been so eager to live fully. Jonathan created in her a true desire for life.

Jonathan as well was quite smitten with Jenny. He'd never known a woman to be so easy to talk to. Usually, most women seemed rather empty and shallow to him. The only commonality was basic primal desires. From there, everything differed. But Jenny, she was different.

She made him feel important the way she watched and listened whenever he spoke. She was like a sponge absorbing everything he gave her. Yet, he didn't feel drained in any way. In fact, he felt as strong as a mountain and as full as the ocean. What he gave to her came back to him in satiating splendor.

She was exquisite. Beauty radiated from every ounce of her body. Sometimes in the evenings when the sun was setting, he could almost swear that a faint glow shimmered around her as she sat in silence, her eyes fixed on his as he bore so easily, all that he dreamed, yearned, and hoped for in life. When Jenny would talk, it was as if angels' wings had brushed his ears. The sound of her voice tickled, charmed, and stroked his male ego. Her knowledge of the world and life urged and challenged him in a new way.

As with everything, the swirling, tantalizing emotions that had been stirred within each of them, slowly took on a new feel. A pulling, intertwining grip had taken hold of their hearts and minds. Jonathan's desire to solve Jenny's past had somehow slipped away. Instead, a need to keep her close willingly replaced any questions of her past.

Jenny had been starved too long for attention. She felt as if every nerve in her body had woken up – sprung to life from a coma. Any physical contact with Jonathan nearly made her heart stop. It was electric. Any unexpected brush or touch of his body overdosed her senses. Causing a gasp of air to rush desperately to her very core. Seeing that gasp of breath intoxicated Jonathan. It made him feel ten feet tall.

Without a word spoken, they both knew they were about to take a step, where there was no turning back. Their mouths spoke of life, but their eyes begged for love. A love that would bind them forever.

Quiet moments began to linger as the need in their eyes overpowered the importance of what they were saying. Each night it grew harder and harder to say goodnight. Often finding themselves up in the wee hours of the morning, each secretly embarrassed for keeping the other up, not wanting to part.

Jonathan, being the gentleman, apologized for being so unthinking about the hour and suggested they retire. "Besides," he said, "it's a bit too chilly out on the porch for you." Jenny, knowing he was right obliged him, though feeling like a child who just had their favorite toy taken away.

As Jenny rose from the swing, a loud shriek startled her and she turned in fright against Jonathan. Just as she realized the noise was only an owl, she also realized her hands were on Jonathan's chest. Frozen, she was also aware that Jonathan's arms were around her. Another moment passed and his arms were still there. Jenny felt lightheaded. As she slowly looked up at Jonathan, she could feel the heat of his arms and chest penetrating her defenses. His eyes were locked on hers. She could hardly breathe. Her body felt electrically charged. With steady unwavering eyes, Jonathan lowered his head toward Jenny. She thought she would faint beneath the touch of his lips on hers. Their kiss was one of love, not demanding, but all-giving.

Jonathan felt drunk with the taste of her lips. Jenny's hands upon his chest were burning a mark upon his heart. He was hers, as if branded. No other woman had claimed his heart so completely.

Jenny slid her hands up around his neck, her body pressed against his. Jonathan's grip grew tighter, feeling their bodies begin to mold together.

"Jenny. . . I. . ." he whispered in a desperate plea.

Without a word, she met his longing gaze, "I know," she said taking his hand and gently leading him inside.

Silently she led him across the floor to the stairs. As she began her assent, she felt a resistant tug on her arm. She turned and saw Jonathan inch back ever so slightly. With a small smile of understanding, she reassured him, "It's okay, Jonathan." His apprehension melted, and Jenny knew there would be no stopping now.

As they ascended the stairs, Jenny could almost feel Jonathan devouring her with his eyes. The heat in his eyes as they ventured along her back made Jenny's heart begin to flutter, and heightened the sensitivity of her body. She quivered as she imagined him watching her every move.

Jonathan was entranced following Jenny as she glided so gracefully up the stairs. The silkiness of her hair, the curves of her neck, the hypnotic rhythm of her hips as they effortlessly ascended the endless staircase. She was truly a vision. He was her slave, her captive. He wanted nothing more than to please her, to quench her desires, mind, body and soul.

Stopping for a moment on the threshold, Jonathan's hand caressingly covered Jenny's before she could turn the knob of her bedroom door. As she turned around and met his gaze, time stopped. Not one word was spoken, yet everything was said in the flash of a promise that glowed in each other's eyes.

Together they turned the knob, opening the door, the last barrier between them. Jonathan then whisked Jenny possessively up into his arms. Jenny touched his lips as if to knowingly seal their vow to each other. Jonathan leaned against the door. The door swung wide as if to say fate has been waiting an eternity – enter your destiny.

The door closes, though the light of a candle could be seen glowing from beneath it. The flame of the candle – miniscule to the fire that burned within. Tonight, Jonathan and Jenny, the intimate sounds of passion and pleasure flowed endlessly for hours, ebbing only as their souls had reached that quintessence of one.

The first rays of sunlight found them peacefully dreaming in each other's arms.

Chapter 20

$\mathcal{J}$enny awoke to the sound of buzzing in her ear. She swatted at her ear to shoo away the annoying intruder. Slowly she opened her eyes. Her heart sank as she began to realize her dream was over. She was back.

Numbly and mechanically, she gathered all her belongings and without glancing back, slowly made herself go home. Exhaustion had a hold over Jenny.

Entering the back door, Jenny dropped everything on the floor. She made tea, went into the front room, grabbed an afghan that was draped over the back of the couch, and turned on her TV. Holding the warm tea close, she looked like a little girl as she curled up in the afghan in the corner of the couch.

For the longest time she sat there, motionless. Her eyes fixed on nothing but thin air. She felt as though her heart had been ripped out the moment she awoke in the forest. She was hurting. Her body ached terribly.

"Weather forecast for tomorrow, Monday, will be a high of 75 degrees, low of 50 degrees, early morning fog may hamper you boaters out there. . ."

"Monday? Tomorrow? What is this? It can't be! I went to the place on Saturday and now it's Sunday? I couldn't have slept through the night there, could I? Maybe that's why I feel so terrible. I wouldn't be surprised if I end up with pneumonia. Well, I'd better make a doctor's appointment in the morning. I don't think Max will mind if I take an hour to see the doctor," Jenny assured herself. "In the meantime, I'd better get myself in bed to play it safe."

She turned everything off and locked the doors before heading upstairs. Jenny was completely out of breath by the time she crawled into bed.

Jenny did not sleep well. Restless dreams kept her tossing and turning most of the night.

The windy hill. The cold and dark halls of the castle. Frantically she ran from room to room. For what, she didn't know. One second she thought she was trying to find her aunt. The next second it was as if she was running away from something harmful. And the next as if she was trying to find her way, for something that would make sense and tell her what to do. "Help me, help me Aunt Abbigale," she moaned, then fell still as a deeper sleep enveloped her.

Morning was hard for Jenny. She felt as if she hadn't slept in a week. Her body ached. Dark circles haunted her eyes. It was almost more than she could do to leave for the bookstore.

At work, Max was concerned about Jenny's health, given her drawn look. "Take all the time you need," he said when Jenny brought up the doctor. "Now git outta here and go take care of yourself."

"Thanks Max, I owe you."

"You owe me nothing child, just get well."

Jenny drove to the doctor's office. Luckily, this was a small town or she'd be waiting all day to be seen. As it was, there were only two people in the office.

"It's a little bit early yet for most of the retired folks around here. . ." the receptionist explained.

Within a half-hour, it was her turn.

"Dr. Farin will see you now, Ms. McBride," called the nurse from the doorway to the examining rooms.

Entering the examining room, the nurse handed Jenny a paper smock.

"Please undress to the waist and put this on. The doctor will be with you shortly." Jenny nodded as the nurse set her chart on the counter, smiled, then left the room.

Jenny had no more finished, when a solid knock on the door startled her. She watched the door begin to open as a deep husky voice asked, "Hello? Ms. McBride?"

"Yes."

Then the door opened just wide enough for a robust old man, clad in doctor whites, to walk into the room.

"Hello, Ms. McBride, my name is Dr. Hank Farin."

"Hello," Jenny said, then with a smile, "for a minute there I thought you were going to say your name was Burl Ives."

The doctor chuckled from head to toe. "You noticed," he began, "the look may be there, but my singing kills the image every time. Want me to sing a few bars? Say, Frosty?"

"No, no, that's quite alright Dr. Farin. I'll take your word for it. Besides, I don't want to start thinking about Christmas. . . winter. . . snow. . . the cold. . ."

"Well then let's get down to business shall we? I understand you aren't feeling well. Is that correct?"

"Yes, it is doctor. I've been feeling a little run down lately. Then yesterday, after several hours of sleep, I was exhausted more than ever."

"You do look rather pale. How's your appetite?"

"Pretty much normal I'd say."

"Stress?"

"Yeah, some, though things have actually gotten better since I moved out here. But I feel worse today than I have in a long time."

"Let me get your temperature and blood pressure."

"Okay, doctor."

Dr. Farin opened the drawer under the counter and removed a white object from it. "How do you like my new toy? Just got this new ear thermometer last week. What a time saver." After a few seconds, "Temperature normal," he announced.

"One down, one to go," Jenny responded.

The blood pressure took a little longer. The doctor released the pressure, frowned, then pumped it back up again.

"Something wrong doctor?", Jenny asked.

"Oh, your blood pressure is a little low."

He continued by taking her pulse, then listening to her heart. Matter of fact, he was listening so intently, Jenny remarked sarcastically, "Waiting for it to talk to you?" He gave a slight smirk, "Oh, it's jabbering up a storm right now." The doctor's smile was definitely gone.

"Is there something wrong, doctor?"

"Are there any health problems in your family, Jenny?"

"No. Not that I know of. . . why?"

"Just curious. I saw in your records that Abbigale Dupree is your aunt. Is that correct?"

"Why yes, she's my mother's sister. . . why do you ask?"

"It's probably nothing, but not that long ago your aunt was in here with similar complaints. Seemed like one minute she was in here as fit as a fiddle the next with her health failing. I told her that if she didn't start feeling better soon, I'd like to send her to the city for tests."

"And. . ?" Jenny prompted.

"Well, I didn't hear back. I assumed she got better. Is she doing better now?"

"I guess so."

"What do you mean by that?"

"She's moved and left me everything. I don't even know how to contact her."

"Now if that don't beat all." The doctor went into silent thought.

"Did you have any idea of what was wrong with her?" Jenny questioned.

"Honestly, I thought her heart was giving out on her."

"And you're saying *mine* is too!"

"Whoa, whoa, Ms. McBride. That's what I thought then. But now that you're exhibiting similar signs, I wonder if it might be hereditary, or possibly something in the house?"

"What's next then, Dr. Farin?"

"I'd like to have you see a friend of mine in the city. He specializes in cardiovascular and pulmonary heart disease. I'd like to rule out any blood or heart disorder."

"I've never had any problems remotely resembling that. Why now? Doesn't that seem a bit drastic?"

"Preventive medicine you might say. But first, I'd like to draw some blood so the test results can be at his office before your appointment."

"When do you want me to see him?"

"I'll have the receptionist call for an appointment while you're getting dressed, then I'd like you to go home and get some rest. Now I mean it, rest, no work. Is that clear?"

"Yes, Dr. Farin."

"I'll get the nurse to draw some blood." The doctor walked to the door, then turned, "Now if you start feeling any worse, you give me a call. Don't you go trying to be your own doctor."

"Okay, I promise."

"Good. I'll go see about that appointment for you. Goodbye."

"Bye, Dr. Farin."

The nurse came and took some blood, then Jenny dressed and headed out to the receptionist.

"Ms. McBride. The appointment Dr. Farin asked me to make is confirmed for tomorrow at 10:30am. The doctor's name is Stephen Tanner. His office address and telephone number are on this card. Do you have any questions?"

"No questions. Thank you," Jenny said taking the card from the receptionist and left the office.

Jenny stopped by the bookstore to tell Max about the doctor's orders.

"No problem Jenny. You go home. It's not like it's Christmas rush on 5th Avenue. I can handle it. Heavens, I've been doing it for years." Max had a comforting smile.

"Thank you Max, but I'm not sure how all this is going to affect my working here. Today an appointment, tomorrow another. . ." Max shushed her.

"One day at a time Jenny. No use looking for trouble. I think you've got enough on your plate to worry about."

"You're right, Max. I'll rest today and see how I am in the morning."

"Sounds like a plan Jenny."

"Actually, I feel a bit better than I did this morning."

"Well, glad to hear it. Before you know it you'll be out painting the town red or whatever the younger folk do around here on their time off."

Jenny said goodbye and took off for home. She actually liked the idea of resting – doing nothing. Driving home she tried not to think about the doctor visit and the upcoming one. Instead, she began to visualize what forms of rest most enticed her.

Going to bed must fall at the bottom of the list. . . rock bottom to be exact. Taking a bubble bath. . . umm. . . okay. What else? Draw, paint, write, read? So many different possibilities. "Who am I trying to fool?" Jenny said, "I know what I want to do. I'm drawn. I don't know how else to explain it. There, lingering in the corners and shadows of my mind. No matter where I go, what I do, or what I say. It's there waiting, slowly drawing me in."

Jenny broke the pull. "Rest! Rest is what he said. But isn't that rest?" The urge was overwhelming Jenny. She retorted, " Rest comes in many forms. You can swim in the lake, draw, paint, whatever you want there. It's a beautiful day. What's the difference if you rest at home or at the place?" Jenny couldn't, or wouldn't argue that. She was a grown woman. It wasn't as if she was going out at night in a rainstorm with only her nightgown on. She'd just be smarter about it. If she wanted to snooze, she'd take her alarm clock with her. Then she'd be sure not to sleep through the night again. She was so out of sorts after the last time. It was a bit creepy.

"Okay, it's settled. Into *the forest of no return*. . . ha ha ha. . ." Jenny joked. Strangely enough, it didn't seem so funny. Somehow it triggered thoughts of the dreams she'd been having about the castle. Something. She just couldn't quite grasp it.

At the house, Jenny put some things together, including the clock, before leaving for the forest. Wasting no time, she was out the back door within five minutes. As the screen door slammed against the door jamb behind her, her mind flashed for a moment to her aunt, as if she were her, walking purposefully into the forest. Slowing for a moment she whispered, "I don't understand, Aunt Abbigale. Help me, please," then continued on into the forest.

Chapter 21

*T*he water was so refreshing. Jenny floated in the pond for an hour, periodically dipping under the surface to invigorate her muscles.

In the background, the radio was playing some hypnotically soothing music by Steven Halpern. It made her feel like she was in her own piece of Heaven. Jenny honestly didn't think she'd be surprised if the birds soaring playfully above would any second turn into angels, not caring to hide their true forms.

Why couldn't life be like this all the time? Uncomplicated, unhurried – just like it seemed in her dreams with Jonathan.

A frown came across Jenny's face, at which point she dove under the water and swam over by the rock. Curiously looking at the rock, Jenny rose out of the water. She slowly circled to the clover side.

"Why is it that I only dream of being with Jonathan when I'm here? Sure, it makes this place extra special, but it's really rather strange. Why don't I dream about him at home? And why haven't I ever dreamt about him before coming here? Maybe there is more to it."

Jenny continued looking over the rock and surrounding clover where she always laid to dream. The rock was really quite beautiful with the shimmery veins running through it. She was about to turn back towards the water when something shiny caught her eye. There, at the base of the rock, just under a small patch of clover. Jenny reached down and picked it up.

It was a locket. A beautiful gold locket, with the letters *A.D.* engraved on the front. Jenny turned the locket over and over in her hand as if trying to get some psychic vibrations off it.

"This must have belonged to my aunt," Jenny uttered in a barely audible voice. With her finger, she gently traced over the engraved letters.

"Aunt Abbigale has been here! There is no question now," Jenny was not able to affirm that this place she had found had been Abbigale and Aaron's place. It was almost uncanny. What were the chances that Jenny should stumble onto *The Place* that Abbigale so frequently mentioned in her journal? It had seemed somewhat far away when read about, but now, with this locket, it was all too real and in some ways invasive, Jenny thought. She felt awkward, as if she had spied into an intimate secret.

She turned the locket over onto its back. Another smaller engraving was on the back. It was a little difficult to read it as if loving hands had worn the ridges, slowly, over time – like a glacier moving down a mountain. The engraving was only understandable because it was one she had heard Aunt Abbigale use, *MTTY BLTT.* Following were the initials *A.V.*

Yes, this was a locket from Aaron, no doubt, and the saying she knew was short for, *I Love You More Today Than Yesterday, But Less Than Tomorrow -- Mitty Blitt.*

Jenny felt sad. All that time her aunt had held onto her love for Aaron. It just wasn't fair. How could Abbigale's father have been so cruel? That has got to be the worst prison a person should have to endure. To have your heart locked away from its true love. Or, maybe that's the wrong way to look at it. Maybe it's locking in what little precious love is left. . . keeping everything else out of reach, for fear of someone trying to strip away what little precious happiness she can still hold close and relive day and day again. . . possibly for all her days.

Tears began to slip down Jenny's cheeks. She felt deeply for her aunt. How could someone so wonderful, so loving, be forced to live without the one person who makes her happy? She deserved so much more. Jenny wiped the tears from her eyes.

Turning the locket onto its side, Jenny pulled at the clasp. Slowly the locket opened. Inside Jenny found a small folded piece of paper. Written on the top was the letter "J." Surprised, Jenny's mind raced. "It couldn't be anyone else. I'm the only "J" in the family. A note for me in Abbigale's locket? This is too weird. It's almost as if. . ." she trailed off as she began to unfold the paper. Jenny realized she was holding her breath by the time she had the note fully in view, and gasped for air.

- *J* -

If to your hand from clover lain,
this note should find its way.
And on this bed of green you stand,
have dreams of love been played.
Then listen well, my child so dear,
They've heard your heart, for they are near.
A head and heart help make a whole,
Not meant to live apart.
There'll come a day, to go or stay,
For between you cannot dart.
So follow your heart, it knows the way,
Then you shall find, what I've found today.

Love you forever,

Aunt Abbigale

Jenny was numb. "How could she know I'd find this? Why did she do this? What does it all mean? Something's not right. . . no. . . that's not it. I think maybe everything's right but in a wrong way." Jenny's head was swimming with the possibilities. She couldn't even begin to answer her own questions. *Whats* and *whys* were flying at her like birds in a feeding frenzy. The only certainty she felt with a growing calmness was that Aunt Abbigale was gone – for good.

Jenny folded the paper so slowly and carefully you'd think she was handling ancient parchment. She slipped the note back inside the locket, then held it tightly in her hand as if trying to absorb it.

In one swift movement, Jenny tossed the locket into her bag, ran straight to the water's edge, and without skipping a beat flew into the water like a dolphin released from captivity, and disappeared beneath the surface. It was only moments before she breached the water's surface, then swam and swam, almost to exhaustion.

Out of the water, Jenny clutched her towel. She wasn't sure what to think. The locket had really thrown in an unexpected twist. "Oh, if only Jonathan were here, he'd know what to do." Jenny was about to continue when a crashing reality stopped her. There would never be a time when Jonathan would be *here*, as she so well put it. This was a dream that would remain a dream forever.

Suddenly Jenny felt emptier than she'd ever felt before. A despair like none other clawed at her heart. "No hope." That's what it was. When you love someone *real* and something goes wrong, you always have some hope, no matter how little or how deep within it lies, that things will work out. But a dream, they are never real to begin with, and reality is the cold empty truth.

Shivering, she dressed. Even though the temperature was still really warm, Jenny wrapped herself in an extra blanket and sat down by the rock, pulling her legs tight against her chest. With her arms hugging her legs, slowly she began to gently rock back and forth.

"Too many things. . . no sense. . . am I finally losing it. . . Aunt Abbigale. . . Jonathan. . . tired, tired, tired. . ." Jenny rocked herself to sleep – a very troubled sleep. She continued to mumble incoherently. After a while, she began to feel a familiar, relaxing tingle.

Jenny fell silent and calm when a warm and gentle hand caressed her cheek and brushed back a lock of hair. Jenny sighed deeply.

"Hey sleepy head, how long are you planning on sleeping?"

Jenny's eyes opened to the sight of Jonathan sitting beside her and smiling down on her. "What?" she said, a little disoriented. Then realizing it *was* Jonathan, she sprang up and embraced him so hard. "Oh Jonathan, don't ever leave me. Please," as tears began to fall.

"What's all this about? I'm not going anywhere. Did you have a bad dream?"

"Dream? I. . . I. . ." she sobbed.

Jenny's fearful embrace softened as Jonathan took over and held her ever so gently, holding her as no man had ever held her. She felt loved. . . safe. . . *home*. Just like the end of the rainbow, the place everyone wonders about. The place where love, happiness and all your desires abound.

No words were spoken for some time. Jonathan just held her.

Jenny began to feel a little silly about the way she had latched onto Jonathan. You know, dream - reality, he doesn't know the difference. It's her dream, her fears, her loss every time she wakes up. Jenny was about to say something, but then, oddly enough, though Jonathan held her gently, he held her with strength. That protective strength a man often displays when they too fear the unknown fate of giving into love.

Jenny looked up at Jonathan, with eyes that would drown a man's soul. That was all it took. From the moment his searing lips

116

touched hers, they were lost. Somewhere between heaven and ecstasy. Breathing only love for each other, and Jenny dreamed on. . .

Her dream seemed so real. Of course, she had lived dreams before. But not quite like this. Without her dreams, her life would surely be a mess. Jonathan was her savior. Her life had not been a very happy one up to this point. She wasn't really the type to contemplate ending her life by suicide, but in all honesty, there had been times she skirted with her safety. Not caring if road conditions were bad, sleeping pills – there were a variety of things one could be careless. . . no. . . *not careful* about. But Jonathan gave her purpose.

As she dreamed their days away, they grew inseparable. They were so much alike. Yet she often relished the gentle strength that radiated from him like the pride of a stag looking down over its domain.

Real life just could never be this way. It was definitely a dream, one that Jenny never wanted to end. Jonathan and Jenny did everything together. Cook, clean, feed the livestock, make repairs, even talk of ideas for improvements. Anything and everything. One day while they were out walking, Jonathan found a chip of Fool's Gold in the shape of a heart and placed it in Jenny's palm, saying, "It is a foolish man who looks at the gold and not the heart. The only purity, the only lasting treasure is the heart. This is our heart – not yours, not mine, but ours. . . to what it has evolved. As foolish as some may think, we understand, don't we?" Beaming, Jenny clutched the stone and kissed his lips as gently as angels' wings.

Jonathan respected her femininity and her intellect. Neither was a threat to him as with so many other men. He didn't keep her from letting her mind soar to the stars in a mixed echo of knowledge and emotions. He just smiled, asked questions, and began to look at things from a new perspective, from new eyes. . . from Jenny's.

Their days together were exciting and full of life. Their evenings were beyond words. If ever two bodies could become one, theirs had, and not with indefinable edges, but with a sharp sparkling, crystal clarity. Sure you've heard of two halves making a whole, the Yin and the Yang. These all seem so infantile, for their bond somehow had transcended where others could only hope to be.

Jenny and Jonathan. Jonathan and Jenny. They were one in the same. Each seeing each other in everything they would say and do. A love one could only dream. . .

Chapter 22

*T*he alarm clock blared loudly. Startled, Jonathan sprang up in his bed. "Nooo!" His heart sank. It was only a dream. . . it was always, only a dream.

Jonathan's heart, which was so light just moments before, was now suffocating in despair. Falling back on his pillow, with his eyes shut tight, Jonathan desperately tried to go back into his dream. It was useless.

He had begun to enjoy sleeping more than his waking hours. These dreams were different. He felt more alive in his dreams than he had ever felt in his whole life. In them, life was worth living, he felt important, a whole man – proud, in control, at ease with himself and most of all for the first time ever, really in love. It was all because of her. . . Jenny. She was truly the love of his. . . what. . . dream? Only a dream. Just a lifesaving thought in a desperate mind.

Jonathan realizing the futility of it all, dragged himself from his bed. He went over to the bedroom window. Drawing the curtain aside, he leaned his forehead against the pane. Outside, the city. Raindrops raced down the glass distorting the shapes of the buildings beyond. Gray upon gray upon gray. The sky, the buildings, the streets, they all blurred together. Each unimportant in itself. Nothing to set one apart from another.

Jonathan had moved to the city five years ago with such high hopes for his future. Things had gone pretty well for a while. He got a job with a well-established law firm. He was on his way. . . or so he thought, until a case he was handling went bad. That's when he learned that "the company" held underhanded tactics and ambition as one in the same. Bottom line – whatever got them the most money.

Jonathan could not conform to their "standards of excellence." He couldn't hurt the people he'd spent so much time learning to help. There was no compromise. Disillusioned, he resigned after four years of hard honest work.

For the last year he had been working at odd jobs in the city's legal offices. A temporary setback he assured himself, until he could decide how or where he would concentrate his efforts. He still wanted to help others, but he wasn't sure yet just how.

Standing in front of the window, Jonathan exhaled long and slow, as the similarity of the rain-smeared view mirrored his tear-drenched soul.

"Enough already! Better fortify those emotional defenses, Jon," he said straightening up and rolling his head to get the kinks out, then continued, "Nothing that a shower and a hot cup of coffee won't cure."

As a lawyer, Jonathan had made a lot of money and had set a sizeable amount of it aside. He could afford to take it a little slow in deciding his future. Jonathan took to partying as well, trying to "enjoy" life. But after a few months that tapered way down. He just couldn't find any decent women. He dated, yet the relationships came and went like the midnight train, with hardly any significance to their passing. Not until Jenny that is. All the single women in the world, and he had to fall for an image of his imagination.

Jenny was like a breath of fresh air to a suffocating, weary man. His dreams of Jenny were different from any of his other dreams. They were so real. But not only real. . . the dreams were like continuing episodes. Sure he's dreamt a dream more than once before, but they were never totally coherent or logical. Also, in normal dreams he would be himself, then someone else, then just a spectator with whole sceneries changing at a moment's notice. No, these were not normal dreams. In these he was always himself, always saw things from an awake perspective.

Jonathan went to the kitchen and made himself a cup of instant coffee. Leaning against the kitchen counter and taking a slug of the coffee, he replayed parts of the dream in his head. "That's another thing," he blurted, "these dreams don't fade from memory". Maybe it'd be better if they did, he thought, as the emptiness reached for him.

"Wow, if only life could really be like that. No city rat race to deal with. No thousands and thousands of people swarming around you every day to make you feel so unimportant." It's funny how a person can find more purpose for life in their dreams than in reality. "I felt like a man. . . strong. . . caring. . . *the protector* . . . important. . . but most of all, loved". A smile crossed Jonathan's face.

The bad thing about these dreams, they were beginning to take over his life. He couldn't wait to sleep and dream. When he'd go to parties now, his thoughts would always drift back to Jenny.

Jonathan tried once or twice to talk to a buddy of his about the dreams, but it didn't take long for him to bag that idea. Hal, his name was, looked at him as if he was losing it. Recommended he see a shrink. Said it must be some insecurity thing or something to do with his job and lousy relationships. So Jonathan kept the dreams to himself, for fear that someone would get the notion to throw him into a padded cell.

His days were becoming more and more mundane. Instead of squaring himself away. . . bucking up. . . he was becoming more resigned to his life. He had never really felt he fit in anywhere. But somehow, he always managed to keep himself going. One thing was for sure though, if given the choice he would chose his dreams of Jenny over everything.

Jonathan finished his coffee and went in to get himself ready for work.

Chapter 23

*J*enny dragged herself home. She was exhausted and out of breath. Just inside the backdoor, she plopped into a chair at the kitchen table. "I guess it's a good thing I'm going to the specialist's tomorrow. I just can't figure it out." Jenny's heart was pounding hard. She put her hand on her chest in an effort to calm her heart and keep it from going into overdrive. "What is wrong with me? I was so relaxed out there and I slept for so long. I should have woken up refreshed even more. But no, I feel horribly drained. I wish Aunt Abbigale had stuck around long enough for the doctor to check her again, or at least to have left some message about her health. Was she really okay when she left? I wish I knew. . ." Jenny's voice faded as she began gazing out the kitchen window, eyes fixed on the forest, mind drifting within the depths beyond.

Jenny was about to lower her hand from her chest when she felt something against her fingertip. She reached inside her top and felt something small and rough. She quickly pulled it out, thinking it a bug or some other unwanted invader, and instinctively threw it on the floor wanting as little contact as possible. Gathering her wits about her, she was finally able to look down at the object of her invasion. "It's the heart stone!

"How? That was in my dream. . ." Jenny was afraid to contemplate any answers, so she just stared at it, dumb-founded. Finally, her intellect kicked in and assumed that she must have picked it up in the moss by the rock while she was sleeping. Somehow it got subconsciously incorporated into her dream. Nonetheless, she liked what it represented to her. She picked it up off the floor.

Jenny just held the stone in her palm – half looking at it and half remembering her dream. "I should put this on a chain, but how? The junk drawer!" She went to the kitchen junk drawer and began clawing through the old remnants of potentially useful items. "This might do it!" She pulled out what looked like a small roll of metal tape. With stone in one hand and tape in the other, Jenny began molding the tape around the heart, pinching it at the top to make a small loop for a chain. "This will work." Having successfully fitted the heart stone for a chain, Jenny held the stone up against her chest, while thoughts of Jonathan poured over her weary body.

Without another thought, Jenny went upstairs and found an old necklace from which she confiscated its chain, and carefully thread it through the loop on the stone. Sleep pulled at her. She placed the necklace on her nightstand. She wanted nothing else but to go to sleep and dream of Jonathan. Shedding her clothes beside the bed, she slipped under the covers.

That night while Jenny slept, an unexpected cold wind howled outside, yet her brow shined with perspiration as she tossed her head from side to side amongst the pillows.

Jenny found herself lying face down on the cold, cracked stone that marked the threshold of the withering, decaying castle. The wind slapped at her face, waking to its frigid sting. Wearily she stood. The doors were only partway open. Not feeling the strength to move the massive doors further, she just barely squeezed within.

Frightened, not really remembering much of the last time she found herself within the bowels of this dying monstrosity, she moved slowly, eyes darting in all directions. Something was wrong here. Everything looked older, somehow more revolting. Chunks of wall and ceiling lay strewn throughout. Then she heard it. . . a slight tinkling sound, followed by a faint muffled tapping noise.

A chill ran down her spine. Jenny felt nauseous. "Oh Jonathan, I need your strength. If only you could save me from this. . . this horrid place," she wished as she carefully stepped over fallen debris, heading in the direction of the sounds. "Maybe I'll find someone who can help me from wherever that noise is coming from." With which, hope sprang into her step. Then she halted abruptly, pressing herself into the shadows against the wall.

"A trap!" Frozen, she didn't know what to do or where to go. If she ran like hell, would she be running away from it, or right into the snarling mouth of it? Panic began to consume her. Then she heard it again. The tinkling sound. Like crystal chimes playing in a gentle breeze. But this time she sensed a faint whisper of her name within the sound, "J-e-n-n-y," so softly.

"Aunt Abbigale? Is that you?" She listened. Only the soft muffled tapping. Whatever it all was or meant, it was coming from somewhere down the corridor. She began to walk, slowly at first. As she moved forward, the tapping sound became more audible. It actually sounded more like the faint slow beat of a heart, except it had a metallic ring to it.

"J-e-n-n-y," followed by tinkling again.

Jenny picked up her step. "Aunt Abbigale! Where are you?" She was walking so quickly that she stumbled over a piece of the rubble hiding in the shadows of the corridor. But she was quick and regained her step.

"J-E-N-N-Y!"

"I'm coming!" she shouted. Just as she was about to take another step, she heard a high-pitched moan as a section of stone broke free from the ceiling, plummeting downward. Jenny dove backwards, falling to the ground just as the stone smashed to the floor only two feet away from her. Dust flew into her eyes. She could feel the bruises beginning where she had hit the hard, debris-ridden floor. She wanted to lie there and cry but knew she couldn't afford the blur of tears in her eyes.

Wiping the dust from her eyes, Jenny strained to see down the corridor. At the end, it went both left and right. Jenny sat up. She felt like she had just slid down a gravel pit — and looked about the same, too. As she brushed some of the dust off herself, a flash of light out of the corner of her eye caught her attention. Down the corridor just for a moment, like sparkling lights, then they disappeared around the corner to the right.

"Jenny. . . you must hurry!"

"I'm coming, Aunt Abbigale. Please wait!"

Jenny got up and quickly moved down the corridor. But even as fast as she moved it seemed to take forever. Sounds of the castle crumbling echoed all around her. Finally, she reached the end of the corridor. She barely glanced left as she knew she had to go right.

There, not more than twenty feet in front of her was a door. Jenny now glanced back to the left corridor, beginning to doubt her choice. She could see nothing within the dark shadows that ruled there. She turned back towards the door. A large part of the ceiling and exterior wall had fallen away, allowing faint light to penetrate and hold back the darkness. With the light Jenny could see well enough to see there was something hanging from the door latch. The wind that also squeezed through with the light made whatever it was, tap the latch plate. "The metal sound," she thought.

Without further hesitation, she walked straight towards the door. Closer and closer. As she reached the door, Aunt Abbigale's locket stared back at her, hanging from the end of the chain on the door latch. As Jenny grasped the locket, the links of the chain fell free of each other and scattered across the floor like pearls from a broken strand.

The locket felt warm in Jenny's palm. She put the locket against her chest as if it could dispel the chill of fear invading her from the decaying, life-ebbing structure in which she would surely be entombed. Then she heard it. A slight tinkling, then yes, it was definitely Aunt Abbigale.

"Jenny," she called, "you must hurry. Come quickly!" Her voice was coming from beyond the door.

Jenny grasped the door latch firmly. Even though it was rusty, with her heightened emotions she turned the latch. Leaning with all her weight against the door, she pushed. It was too hard. The door jamb must have shifted with all the crumbling of the walls and. . . a loud cracking sound from overhead gave Jenny a start as she realized more of the ceiling was going to give way any second. BOOM! The sound was deafening. Jenny could feel the falling debris graze her as she fell through the doorway.

It was dark. She couldn't see.

"Jenny my dear child, you must hurry." Abbigale's voice echoed from somewhere.

"But where, Aunt Abbigale?" Jenny sobbed.

"Jenny, the locket – it holds the answers you seek."

Jenny realized the locket wasn't in her hand anymore. She must have dropped it when she fell through the door. "Where is it? I've lost it!" She began groping the floor around her. Forward she crawled on her hands and knees. The rubble that had fallen just outside the door blocked most of the light. The dust obscured the rest.

Jenny could hear the sounds of cracking, hissing, and groaning as the room began to lose its hold on the ground where it had stood for so many years. Just as Jenny was beginning to fear there was no hope, a faint glow caught her eye. It looked as if something was reflecting what little light could still make it through the door. As quickly as she could, Jenny made her way over to it. With every movement she could hear the crumbling stone hit like pellets on the floor. Even the floor was shifting now. An enormous crack moved her feet in opposite directions.

"Jenny, it's now or never," she heard Abbigale cry out.

Jenny lunged for the object, hoping with all her heart that it was the locket. It was! With both hands around it, she held the locket tightly against her chest.

"It's time Jenny." Abbigale's voice sounded calm and soothing now.

From nowhere, twinkling lights began to appear from all around Jenny. A feeling of great love and compassion flowed through her as the lights encircled her. She could no longer hear the sounds of the dying castle. It was as if it had disappeared – just fallen out of existence. She was very lightheaded. No longer in a raging storm, but somewhere gentle and soft, as if floating through the clouds on a warm summer's day. Such immense joy she felt. As the clouds began to part, she could glimpse a golden field below. It looked familiar.

Jenny's sleep became more restful and calm. She was no longer tossing but rather smiling. Quietly she muttered, "Jonathan, I'm coming."

Chapter 24

The warm glow of early morning sun bathed Jenny's eyes, slowly bringing her awake. As her eyes opened, she remained motionless, for her body felt as if it had melted into the bed. She felt so relaxed. "Jonathan," the word echoed in her mind. She had dreamt of him, only this dream was a little different. Jenny gently tried to coax her mind into remembering her dream because even though she felt good now, she also couldn't shake a feeling of impending doom.

As she lay still, her eyes ebbing open then closed, pieces of her dream returned. The castle. . . the fear of not knowing what to do. . . where to go. Then Abbigale, how odd that was. "I remember the locket. I thought for sure I was going to die! I'd lost the locket. Abbigale said to hurry – it held the answers. Oh how I needed Jonathan. Then, I remember finding the locket, grasping it for dear life not knowing why, but I trusted my aunt. I could swear the world that had surrounded me crumbled away, yet I did not. The white sparkling lights – it was as if they protected me. Then I don't know how much time had passed, but I remember seeing Jonathan's fields."

Jenny began to have difficulties remembering all the pieces. "I know I saw Jonathan, but it wasn't at all like my other dreams with him. It all seemed too surreal, disjointed, just flashes of times we shared."

It was no use trying to recall anymore now. It was all fading. Maybe she'd remember some more later. Jenny's trailing thought went back to the locket. "What is it about the locket?" She rolled over towards the night table. There it lay, like a Leprechaun hiding its gold – what secret did it hide?

Jenny got out of bed, showered and dressed. Before leaving the bedroom she placed the locket in her pocket – it had become almost a security blanket at this point. For good luck, she then placed the stone necklace around her neck.

Her appointment with the specialist was today. She was surprised to see it was only 7:30am when she got down to the kitchen. It felt much later. Jenny fixed a light breakfast – a couple pieces of toast and some apple juice. She wasn't feeling very good. She didn't feel tired, just queasy. Sitting at the kitchen table, her gaze again became transfixed on the forest beyond the window.

"Why only there?" she thought. "I don't understand why the dreams of Jonathan seem so real when I'm in that place, yet here, it seemed no different than other dreams. Maybe it's because it's not nighttime. . . yeah. You know, daydreaming, that must be the difference, you're more intellectually awake when you daydream. Therefore, your mind makes more of an effort to make it seem real!" Great, now Jenny you've become a scientist with expertise in the area of dream states. Maybe you'd be *smarter* to check out Max's to see if he has any books on the subject. I know you think highly of your analytical and deductive reasoning, but. . . give me a break, will ya? Fine! Jenny conceded. It'll give me something to read while I'm waiting for the doctor.

Jenny finished eating, still not feeling real great. After washing her dishes, she paused again to look at the tall trees guarding the forest edge. She reached into her pocket and pulled out the locket, and then removed the paper inside. "You know finding the locket there was weird, but a note addressed to me inside? This would be a good one for *Unsolved Mysteries*. They'd be more likely to know what they're doing. Us amateurs have a tendency to go in circles a lot and never accomplish anything." Jenny huffed when the first thought of an amateur circling was a dog chasing its tail.

Jenny unfolded the note carefully and began to read from the top. . . "No! I don't have time for this." She folded the note and placed it back inside the locket. "I have an appointment to get to. I can look at this later." She was out the door within five minutes.

She drove down to Max's bookstore. He was opening the shop just as she arrived.

"Jenny," Max elated, "I'm glad to see you. Are you feeling any better?"

"Yeah, thanks for asking."

"What are you doing here this morning?"

"I've got an appointment in the city and I thought I'd get a book to help pass the time while waiting."

"Good idea, anything in particular?"

"Nah, just think I'll browse for a while."

"Well, have at her, girl. You know pretty much where everything is."

"Okay. Thanks Max."

Jenny didn't want to tell Max she was looking for a particular type of book. He might think her a bit strange if she started acting like evaluating dreams was of any great importance to her. He might wonder if she had some kind of cultist plans in the making, heaven forbid! You know how some people get when you start reading on unfamiliar subjects. All of a sudden you become one of *them*, whatever that all is supposed to mean.

"Okay Max, I got one."

"Good."

Jenny handed him the book and glanced up at the clock. "Oh my goodness, I didn't realize how long I've been here. I've got to get going Max – my appointment!"

"Here you go, Jenny. You know, it's kind of funny. . ." Max was looking at the cover as he handed it to her.

"What's funny?" Jenny responded defensively – ready for the interrogation.

"You and your aunt are very much alike."

"What do you mean Max?"

"To put it bluntly, she read this book too."

"Really? That doesn't seem to be the type of thing I would expect her to read."

"Then you ought to look at her file sometime. The kind of books she read for the last few months before she. . . left town. This one is mild compared to some of the others."

"What do you mean?"

"Not that I've read this but, the title, it sounds okay – possible. But some of the one's Abbigale read, well, you'd never expect. . ." With a strange expression on his face, Max seemed to drift off into deep thought.

"Oh my gosh, I got to go Max," remembering her appointment.

"Okay kiddo. Drive safely." Max blurted, having snapped back from wherever his thoughts had taken him.

"I promise Max. I'll check in with you later, after my appointment."

"I'd like that Jenny. I worry about you."

"I care about you too, Max. See ya!"

With that, Jenny was out the door. Max stood at the window and watched as she drove off down Main Street and out of town. Max sighed. A sad expression fell across his face. He turned away from the window.

Chapter 25

*A*t his kitchen table, Jonathan sat silently staring into his coffee cup as if it were a wishing well, hoping to get some answers to the torment he was living in.

"I'm pathetic. I choose a dream over reality. I need to get my head together. Maybe this is my mind's idea of a wakeup call. Logical analysis is what's needed here. . ." Jonathan sipped at his coffee.

"I can't pretend anymore. This city job isn't for me. It's time to cut my losses. I'm not doing anyone any favors staying here. But, where do I go? What work will I do? You know, at this stage of my life even the Peace Corps is somewhat of a tempting idea. . . a little extreme maybe, but more in the right direction. A small town out in the country?"

His thoughts drifted back to the farm he had dreamed of so many times. . . and her face. "Oh Jenny, maybe you are really out there somewhere. Could these dreams actually be more like a premonition of what is to come?" Jonathan stopped himself. Premonition, heck, that's impossible. It would be one thing if he saw himself with Jenny on a farm in the country, but this – we're talking about cowboys and the Wild West! Going back in time just doesn't fit the bill here. We're talking the impossible. . . unless of course you live on the THX screen!

One last gulp and the coffee was gone. "I'm going to do it! I'll turn in my resignation today," he proclaimed, setting his cup back firmly on the table for emphasis. "I know I'm making the right decision. I'm not sure how or why I know this, but I can feel it in my gut."

With that, Jonathan got ready for work, already formulating his resignation letter and shpiel. Within the half-hour, he was out of his place and on his way to the bus stop.

Standing there at the corner, there was a new air of strength and confidence about him. Maybe he was just standing taller, or maybe he was finally standing confidently again.

Movement from the corner of his eye drew his attention toward the approaching bus. Jonathan took a deep breath as he stepped on. He was ready.

Chapter 26

*J*enny felt like a dumb tourist. She certainly wasn't driving with much savvy. The address wasn't all that easy to find as she had anticipated. For some reason, the traffic wasn't very understanding of her lack of geographical familiarity.

"Honk!" "Beep!" "Hey Lady! Peddle faster will ya?" Man, how embarrassing. "I can't believe I'm helping the male gender prove that women don't know how to drive."

Finally, she spotted the building. "Thank you!" she blurted, "Okay, now parking." Of course she had to drive two blocks away before she luckily found a parking spot. Actually, it more realistically found her, for she had to slam on her brakes to avoid hitting the car that bolted out of the spot.

Jenny couldn't help but feel a sigh of relief as she turned Kit's engine off. "Sorry to put you through all this torture, Kit. At least you can rest awhile. I'll be back in a little bit." Jenny patted Kit's nose as she headed off towards the specialist's office. "Tanner? Right?" she quizzed herself.

"Yuck." She just didn't feel good. The butterflies were already starting to churn. "What will they find out?" She pondered. Her rhetorical side couldn't pass up this opportunity, "Well, if you knew what they'd find, you'd have no reason to be here now, would you?" Jenny took a deep breath. "I just have to chill out. Think about something else —*not!*"

Jenny arrived at Dr. Tanner's office twenty minutes early. After checking in with the receptionist, she sat down in the lobby and pulled out the book she got at Max's, *Dreams: Myths, Theories and Facts.*

Hmm, she thought, as she opened the book and turned to the contents page. A good portion of the book covered the history of dream research – seemed to be pretty dry reading. If she hadn't been more interested in getting an answer to a specific question, she might be more likely to read it.

History was followed by more defined types of research. Testing modern theories and the factual results. Jenny glazed through the different theories. Nothing like she was looking for. Most of the research dealt with electrode responses during sleep tests.

"Nah, there might be something embedded in the clinical jargon, or maybe somewhere in the section about dream effects on the physical body, but. . ." she continued to thumb through the pages. "What I'm looking for has to be in the myths section if anywhere."

Jenny sat and intently scanned the pages, looking for anything close to stand out. "Dreams and their relation to premonitions. . . subconscious and the inner voices. . ." Still nothing. "Oh, here's a good one, it says dreams are really reality and reality is really our dreams. Whoa! That's a mind bender. I mean think about it for a second. In my case that would be great. I could be with Jonathan. . . wait. . . maybe I'd be in that old castle instead!" Jenny shuddered at the thought. She read on.

"Miss McBride?" The receptionist called.

Jenny looked up. "Yes," she said, putting her book away.

"The doctor is ready to see you. If you'll just come this way, please."

Jenny got up and followed the receptionist to an examination room.

"Do you prefer to go by Jennifer or Jenny?"

"Jenny is fine."

"Okay Jenny, Dr. Tanner is finishing with another patient right now. He'll be in shortly."

"Thank you," Jenny mechanically replied.

With that, the receptionist put her file in the slot on the outside of the door and pulled it closed behind her. Suddenly, Jenny felt very alone. She contemplated reading more of her book, but, certain she couldn't find the answers she wanted, decided there wasn't enough time before the doctor came in.

The examining room was so impersonal. It seemed to be coming alive, as if it had conscious thought. One moment a room – now it was as if she were in the belly of a cold, heartless executioner, the air thick with its anticipation of the destruction of yet another helpless soul. Would the room devour her with the truth of some fatal disease?" It mocked her. The cold stainless steel, the needles, the swabs. . . she was getting nauseous.

Stop it. Stop it. "STOP IT!" the last she blurted out loud. "I must stop doing this to myself. Take a deep breath." She tried to calm herself with several long, deep breaths. It helped. . . sort of.

A knock at the door startled Jenny. "Yes?"

With her response, the door opened and in walked a man in his late forties. Tall, thin, with dark hair. His eyes were almost as cold as the room. His face and movements showed the pressure of the city pace. She didn't like the feeling. It was like an omen. He smiled, but it appeared to be such an effort, as if he'd learned it in "Bedside Manner 101." I'll bet he flunked that class, Jenny chuckled to herself, attempting to rid herself of those lousy thoughts.

"Miss McBride. . . Jenny is it?"

"Yes"

"I'd like to get right to it here. I've talked with your doctor. He forwarded your blood samples to me."

"And?" Jenny pushed a little rudely in return.

"Relax Jenny. We've just begun here. You sound like the case is closed already."

"Sorry. Guess I've always been the pessimist – not the optimist. Continue, please, Dr. Tanner."

"There are a few tests I'd like to do and then we should have a good idea of which direction to take."

"Okay. Could you explain the tests to me?"

"Certainly"

The doctor went through naming and describing the various tests to Jenny, taking care not to delve too much into the *whys* for the tests. As he continued, Jenny's hand gently fidgeted with the stone around her neck. Somehow, it just made her feel closer to Jonathan, and right now, she could certainly use some of his strength.

"Now, unless you have any questions, I'd like to get started"

"No. I don't think so."

"Then, I'll get the nurse in here to get you ready."

"Okay" Jenny said hesitantly.

The doctor walked out. Jenny let out a deep sigh. From her pocket, she pulled out her aunt's locket. She took the note from inside and reread it again.

- *J.* –

If to your hand from clover lain,
This note should find its way.
And on this bed of green you stand,
Have dreams of love been played.
Then listen well, my child so dear,
They've heard your heart, for they are near.
A head and heart help make a whole,
Not meant to live apart.
There'll come a day, to go or stay,
For between you cannot dart.

So follow your heart, it knows the way,
Then you shall find, what I've found today.

Love you forever,

Aunt Abbigale

Without a word, her mind swimming in the search for the meaning behind the note, she folded and placed it back inside the locket. It was none too soon, for as she put it away the nurse came in.

Jenny was subjected to a variety of tests. She was tired and wanted to go home. Finally, the tests were over and she found herself back in her examination room, waiting for the doctor to return. She wanted him to hurry up, but then she wanted him never to come back. She sat in a chair in the corner of the room. It was easier to lean her head against the wall and catch a few Zzs.

It seemed like forever, but the doctor finally returned.

"Well?" Jenny said as he came into the room. He didn't answer right away, so now she was on edge.

"The results of the tests were productive."

"Productive? What does that mean?"

"Now Jenny, you need to relax here and let me talk."

Jenny felt scolded. She shrunk back into her chair. "Alright, doctor, talk away." He definitely frowned at her sarcastic remark, though he didn't acknowledge it further.

"As I was saying. . . the tests were productive, but not conclusive. Your condition. . ."

Jenny cut him short, "Please Dr. Tanner, no long drawn out words. Give me the basic facts."

The doctor's gaze was intense for a moment. "Okay. . . no frills." Jenny nodded. "There are definite indications of an accelerated deterioration in that your heart isn't. . . shall we say. . . pulling its share of the workload."

"Uh-h, I don't think I'm following you. . . exactly. . ."

"We can't find any abnormalities, any blocked or dysfunctional areas in your circulatory system, yet. . . your heart is not putting out the effort needed to maintain your body. An analogy to help you picture this better would be like a plant that gets less water every day, with less nutrients in it. Slowly the plant deteriorates until. . . it stops."

"Until *what*? It withers and *dies*?"

"That is the analogy to a point. Just as with a plant, you can give it more water and added nutrients. So can we in the medical profession do with people."

"So you can give me some medication to take care of this then?"

"It's not that simple, in your case."

"What do you mean?"

"We have to be extra careful what methods we determine to use for you. Medication will of course be the last option here."

"Why do you say that? What's so different about my case?" Jenny pushed defensively.

"I'm not saying we won't try some form of medication down the road. And no, you are not so different than anyone else."

"Well then what, doctor!"

"You must know Jenny, as a physician we have to take into account the effects the medication will have on the fetus."

"*Fetus!*"

"Why yes, Jenny. Why are you looking at me like that?"

"You're saying I'm *pregnant*?" Jenny laughed, half hysterically.

"I'm sorry, I thought you knew."

The apology for his error not comforting her at all, "No that's impossible! I haven't been with anybody. . . except. . ." Jenny stopped short. No, no, no. . . he's a dream – remember?

"You must be wrong, doctor."

"Jenny, I'm sorry but your blood test was definitely positive."

Jenny didn't hear much else. She became like a zombie – nodding, agreeing, not caring.

Before she knew it, the doctor was escorting her back up to the receptionist.

"Now, I'd like to schedule an appointment for next week," the doctor continued with his I'm-in-a-hurry exit formalities.

"Oh, yes, yes, okay." Jenny responded, realizing she hadn't heard a word he'd said.

"If you have any questions, please feel free to call back. By next week we should have a good balanced regime ready for you."

"Yeah, okay Dr. Tanner. Whatever you say."

"Jenny, are you alright?" He looked at her puzzled.

"Yeah, just trying to soak all this in."

"I'm sorry for the blunt comments about. . . I thought you knew. . . I'm terribly sorry." The doctor stumbled over his words.

"You didn't know. It happens, I guess."

Feeling somewhat redeemed, the doctor put his hand on Jenny's shoulder. "It'll all work out just fine. You'll see." With that, he patted her shoulder, said goodbye, and returned back down the hallway.

"This just can't be. I must be dreaming. I don't understand."

"Ms. McBride?"

"Yes?" Jenny acknowledged.

"What would be a good day for you next week?"

"You know. . . can I check my schedule first and call you back to make an appointment? I really just can't think about that right now."

"Well, if you must," the receptionist remarked, somewhat put off, "but don't wait too long. We must get you scheduled, and the doctor is a very busy man. His schedule fills up fast. . ."

Jenny interrupted, "Yes, yes, I'm aware of that. I appreciate your concern, but I will have to call you back."

"Very well, here is the doctor's card." The receptionist handed the card to Jenny and with that, she was out of there.

Outside the doctor's office, Jenny leaned against the wall.

"Please, please, please. . . someone, anyone, how can this be? I must be dreaming."

But she knew she wasn't.

Chapter 27

$\mathcal{I}$t wasn't as easy as Jonathan thought – telling his boss he was quitting.

Too late now – not that he'd change his mind if he had it to do over again. He knew he had done the right thing. A tremendous weight had been lifted off his shoulders.

Within a few hours, Jonathan had all his pending work passed on to other co-workers and all his personal belongings gathered up. He didn't have much to take with him. Most fit into his briefcase, the rest into a small box he could carry under his arm.

He said his good-byes making his way out the door. He left without looking back.

Another chapter closed. Another beginning – but what direction, he thought?

A moment of uncertainty was quickly squelched by the image of Jenny's face, warm and bright in his mind.

"I may never find you Jenny, you may not even exist out there, but you exist in my heart and right now, that's what will keep me going forward. For in a way, you are with me, even if it's only in my dreams."

Jonathan walked outside the office building and down the street to his bus stop.

The whole way, all he could think of was Jenny. The hours and days he had spent with her. The funny things she'd said. How she captivated his attention any time she spoke. He never tired of listening to her sweet, sweet voice. She made him feel so alive.

He ached to be close to her now. Remembering the oneness he shared with her – euphoria wouldn't do the feeling justice.

Squealing brakes broke his train of thought – his bus.

Jonathan stepped onto the bus, stopping briefly to look back down the city street he'd walked so many times.

The bus continued on its route down through the city – Jonathan's face looking out the window to somewhere beyond the streets that passed.

Chapter 28

*J*enny was having a hard time focusing. *I need to sit for a minute. I can't deal with this and concentrate on anything else, let alone driving home.*

"Hot dogs! Ice cold drinks!"

Jenny turned toward the vender's call.

A hot dog stand just around the corner ahead, and off to the side was a shady tree with a bench underneath.

Jenny made a beeline for the bench. No one was sitting at it now and it seemed like her only option at the moment. She dropped onto the bench.

"Hot dogs! Hot dogs!" the vender's voice enticed.

Jenny put her hand on top of her head. "What? I mean, do I have an 'X' on the top of my head I don't know about? I don't feel anything up there. You know, it's like 'X' marks the spot, dump everything here!" she quietly mocked herself. "Yep, definitely a candidate for *Unsolved Mysteries*. I think I have just about filled the bill for one whole show," she sighed, "Jenny, you are pathetic."

Jenny closed her eyes. *Maybe if I can just relax here for a moment. Things can't be as bad as they seem.*

The early afternoon sun took some of the edge off the chill that had crept over Jenny. "Just don't think. . . don't think about anything."

The street sounds faded as she forced her mind into neutral. Not only were the shouts of the street-side vender becoming indistinct, but even the sounds of the approaching city bus.

Chapter 29

*J*onathan began to mentally continue making plans for his exodus from the city. *Things are going to get better. I'll do it all right this time. I'll think it all through before leaping.*

You could almost see the gears cranking in his head. He may have been facing the window, but he wasn't paying attention to the sights as they passed. He felt his confidence coming back and the beginning of renewed desire for the future, and what it might hold.

The brakes screeched as the bus stopped at the signal.

"Hot dogs! Ice cold drinks!"

The almost instant smell of grilled hot dogs awakened Jonathan's senses by way of his stomach.

"Where is that delicious smell coming from?" He questioned, his eyes having difficulty pinpointing the source immediately due to the sun's glare.

As the signal turned green, Jonathan found the hot dog stand. Seeing those hot dogs glisten as they turned on the grill made his mouth water.

Just as he was about to turn his head back forwards, something shiny caught the sun's rays and Jonathan's attention. Under the tree on the bench. On the neck of a. . . he strained to see between the passing people. . . a woman. The hair began to stand up on the back of his neck. He knew it wasn't possible, yet. . . he stretched in his seat to see.

"Too many people in the way. Move! I have to see!" The bus began to pick up its speed.

"No!" All he could get were flashes of sight, just like trying to see with a strobe light flashing on and off – always a second too short to tell. In a second he'd be past. She, whoever she was, would be gone from sight. Just as he thought all was lost, the crowd cleared, but now her head was down!

"Look up, look up!"

Chapter 30

*J*enny was beginning to get relaxed when a big man plopped down on the bench next to her, jolting her back to reality. The smell of exhaust fumes bellowed through the air. Jenny coughed on its taste.

Those stinky busses, she thought, as she looked up to see the bus passing on the street in front of her.

Jonathan was frozen – face and hands glued to the glass.

"She. . . she's. . ."

Then he saw it shine again, he looked at her neck. . . Fool's gold . . . a *heart*!

He looked up at her face again, only to see shock mirrored in her eyes.

Without a moment's notice, fantasy collided with reality.

Jenny couldn't breathe – Jonathan couldn't move. Yet, the bus drove on. Neither realizing the distance growing between them until it was too late.

Cross traffic, pedestrians, anything and everything that could possibly block their sight. Eye contact severed, both regained a small form of coherency.

Jenny sprang from the bench as she watched the bus turn a corner up ahead.

"Kit, Kit! I have to follow the bus – at least try!" She ran all the way to the car bouncing off oblivious pedestrians unaware of her desperate flight. By the time she reached Kit, she was gasping for air. "Gotta go, gotta go, hurry, hurry!"

Jenny whipped Kit out of the parking space so fast she just barely missed a small Fiat in her lane. Luckily, the Fiat's brakes were good, which is more than you could say about the driver's verbiage. Jenny didn't care. Nothing mattered but catching that bus.

Jonathan couldn't believe it. "I've got to get off this bus and get back there!"

He pleaded with the bus driver to no avail.

"I'm sorry sir, but we have our rules. No letting passengers off between stops. If we did that, we'd have people stopping us every ten feet. . ." the driver rambled on.

Jonathan could only look back out the rear window, his heart sinking further and further as the distance between them grew greater and greater.

By the time the bus reached the next stop, Jonathan was in such a frenzy he was practically pulling at the doors to get out even before the bus came to a full stop.

"Hey mister! You break them, you'll pay!" the driver growled.

"So sue me!" Jonathan said as the doors opened.

He bolted off the steps and onto the sidewalk, not even aware he'd left his belongings back under his seat.

The bus driver grumbled as he rounded another corner – glad to be rid of him.

"She can't be gone. Please don't let her be gone."

Jonathan's hope was diminishing, realizing how long it was going to take for him to get back there. Just then he saw an alleyway ahead. "Yes! This will save me some time."

Jonathan turned into the alleyway being quickly swallowed by its shadows, just as Jenny drove frantically past the alleyway and down the street he'd left, looking for Jonathan's bus.

"This is no good." Jenny cried. "How will I ever find that bus? His bus? I didn't even see the number. What route does it take?" Jenny continued down the street, hoping the bus had a basic straight route.

At the end of the alleyway, Jonathan almost took out an old lady as he flew out onto the sidewalk. Traffic didn't look too thick. "Maybe I can cut across the street," the words barely finished as he quickly tried to calculate.

Finding what he thought was a good opportunity, he jumped out into the street, only he didn't see the closing car hidden by the parked Loomis truck.

The further down the street Jenny drove, the more she became aware of how many side streets she had passed, any one of which the bus could have turned on.

She began to slow Kit down, as it got harder to see with welling tears about to stream down her face.

In the faint distance, emergency sirens could be heard, but Jenny was unaware of them due to the pain she was feeling, as she drove out of the city in deep despair.

Chapter 31

The drive back was difficult for Jenny. It took everything she could do to maintain some sort of focus on the road ahead.

"The road. . . just concentrate on the road," she warned herself.

No radio blared this time in the car. Jenny already had more than enough to occupy her mind.

The further she drove from the city, the more everything that had happened seemed to blur together into one nightmarish hoax, with her as the victim.

"I don't understand any of this. Wake up Jenny! This has to be a horrible nightmare. It's all too preposterous!"

Jenny had to shift in her seat feeling a sharp pinch from inside her pants' pocket.

The locket, she thought.

Wiggling her fingers into the pocket, she retrieved the pain-inflicting culprit. Holding the locket in her hand conjured up thoughts of the riddle on the note inside.

Hmmm, Jenny pondered.

"I didn't think much about it at the time, all things considered, but the comment Max made about being so much like Aunt Abbigale – he had referred to her account card.

A new interest perked in Jenny's mind. "I have to go there when I get back. It may be nothing, but I have to know. Why would Max mention it unless there was a memorable connection – something that was different or unusual. Oh, Aunt Abbigale," Jenny prayed, "you must help me to understand."

Kit, as if aware of the importance of time, flew down the road like a kite in a windstorm.

Jenny pulled into town at about 4pm. She headed directly for Max's bookstore.

Max was quite surprised to see Jenny.

"Hey, young lady. What are you doing back here? I didn't expect you to come by. I figured at most you'd call."

"It was a last minute decision. On my way back I got to thinking about what you said to me about my aunt."

"What? You mean the similarities between the two of you?"

"Sort of. More the bit of how I should look at her account card."

"Oh. . ."

"Do you mind if I have a look at it?" Jenny smiled sheepishly.

"I don't see why not. Let me go get it." Max turned and walked over to the files. "So how did your appointment go? Everything okay?"

Jenny was glad Max was facing the other direction when he asked that question. He didn't see the initial cringe on her face, or the awkward fidgeting as she responded.

"They just ran a bunch of tests. The results won't be back for a couple days. Other than that – not much. The doctor didn't seem too concerned." Right. . . she thought to herself, talk about stretching truths to their limits. Results of some of the tests would be back in a few days, but one biggie was already in. As for the doctor's display of not being too concerned, that was more likely due to his lack of bedside manner.

Max returned with the card. "Here, take a look. Bet you'd never guess in a million years that Abbigale would read these kinds of books." He handed her the card.

"I'm gonna grab a cup of coffee for myself. You wanna cup?"

"No thanks, Max," Jenny replied concentrating more on the card.

"Suit yourself," Max commented as he disappeared into the back of the store.

"Wow, I don't believe this. . ." Jenny's said, her surprise escaping her.

The majority of the card was as you'd expect for an elderly woman, but then, towards the end, a drastic change. Jenny read those entries: *Dreams and What They Mean, Paranormal Encounters, Fairies, Pixies and other Mystical Creatures.* The last entry – *Parallel Time, Worm Holes, and Time Travel.*

"And I was worried about getting the book on dreams. She beats me hands down!"

"Hey, Max."

"Whatcha need?" Max answered.

"Are there anymore cards, or is this it?"

"That's it," he said as he emerged from the back, "but you know what I find really strange?" he said pointing on the card. "See here, all these books up here on the card were read over several years' time. But these last ones, they were all within a two-week period."

"I see what you mean. So you're saying she didn't get any more books from you after these?"

"Nope, nada!"

"Did you ever try to find out why she was suddenly so interested in these books?"

"Didn't really get much of a chance."

"What do you mean, Max?"

"It wasn't until that last one she got that I guess it sunk in – the oddity of it all. I planned on asking her about it the next time I saw her. Figured maybe she had watched some movie that piqued her fancy. Maybe she thought she had been abducted by aliens, had a close encounter, or something along those lines. You never know these days. . . no offense intended."

"So, did you ask her?" Jenny prodded.

"Never saw her again. Not in the store, on the streets, nowhere!"

"Huh?" was all she could muster. Jenny handed the card back to Max. "Thanks, Max. I've got a hunch that this is all going to make sense. . . things are beginning to align like tumblers in a lock."

"What do you mean by that Jenny?"

"Oh nothing really," she said, knowing perfectly well that was far from what she meant. She could feel it, like a puzzle, things were starting to take shape. She just couldn't tell what shape yet. Thoughts were shooting through her head faster than she could logically think. She had to get out of there to sort it all through.

"Max, I've got to run now."

"Okay Jenny, just take care of yourself."

"I will Max, thanks."

With a smile, she headed for the door.

Max wasn't so sure. He tried not to let on, but he knew Jenny was holding back. Something was definitely not right with her. He sighed silently, shaking his head. He watched Jenny walk out the door. "What is that girl up to?"

Chapter 32

At home, Jenny went straight for the bookshelves. "I'm sure I looked at all the titles. I don't remember seeing any of those books." She looked at each shelf, then started scouring the house. "If only I could find them, maybe there would be a clue – anything that might make sense of all this."

Jenny searched in vain. Upstairs, downstairs, it didn't make a difference. Those books were nowhere to be found.

The longer Jenny looked and re-looked, she knew she'd never find them. At the same time, she began to realize she'd never see her aunt again. Not that she didn't want to see her, rather, it wasn't possible.

Jenny's subconscious seemed to be well ahead of her conscious thought. She was desperately trying to use the left side of her brain and make sense of everything, yet, the right side kept whispering things, possibilities, *what ifs.*

Finally, Jenny slowly dropped to the floor in the middle of the upstairs hallway, her eyes unfixed, her mind a jumble. She wanted desperately to stop thinking, but thoughts and words poured relentlessly through her mind. Abbigale had stayed at the Dupree house because of her love for Aaron. . . she just walked into the woods and never came back. . . *The Place*. . . the dreams of Jonathan. . . a heart condition – like Abbigale? . . . the decaying castle dreams. . . the locket. . . pregnant. . . Jonathan. . . Round and round, a kaleidoscope of hopes, fears, uncertainties, all overlapping, twisting, turning, blending in a sea of endless motion.

"STOP!" Jenny shouted. "Enough already!" Tears were streaming down her cheeks. "I don't know how much more I can take of this."

Picking herself up off the floor, she instinctively walked to the kitchen sink, got a glass of water, and looked questioningly towards the forest as she sipped the water – her tears subsiding. Jenny stood silently watching, trying not to think at all. Slowly she began to relax.

Shadows of the house began to stretch toward the forest. Daylight was ebbing. Jenny looked down at the way the shadows distorted the house more and more. What once looked like the shadow of a house now looked more like the shadow of an ominous fort – or maybe a. . . castle?

Just then Jenny thought she saw flickering lights in the forest edge. It was so quick. She reached over the sink and opened the kitchen window for a better view. The wind had picked up a bit. She could smell a dampness in the air. It made her shiver.

"There!" Back in, maybe fifteen feet or so. It was darker back there than at the edge of the forest. "What is it? Almost looks like fireflies. But at this distance they wouldn't be that bright." The lights seemed to stretch out in a line, careful not to come too close to the forest edge. Jenny watched as the lights playfully danced. "My own personal light show. This is great!" She even giggled a few times watching the lights in their Ping-Pong off-the-wall antics. Jenny was a second away from running out to join in the fun, when just as quickly as they came, they filtered back into the deeper forest. Two, then one little light flashed as it zipped over the brush behind the others, then nothing. Sadness crept back into Jenny. "Where were they going?"

Images of the lights floating through the forest to *The Place* mesmerized her tired mind. She mentally watched as they entered *The Place* and, after a few moments of artful maneuvers, nestled gently into the moss in front of the rock.

"What?" Jenny was startled by her visual imagery. "Why did they go there? Was it me thinking it, or something else letting me know it?" She stopped to think about it for a moment. "Jenny, you are really losing it, girl!" The realization raised a smirk from Jenny. She remembered sensing or seeing sparkling lights once. . . before she dreamt about Jonathan. . . out there. . .

"More and more I'm beginning to think logic doesn't apply here." Silently standing at the window and watching the forest, she lovingly ran her hand across her belly.

Chapter 33

*I*t was almost 6pm. Jenny wasn't hungry. "I know. . . I'll watch some TV. I can always veg out doing that – it's a real no brainer." Jenny went into the front room, turned on the tube and remembering. . . gently plopped into the chair. She couldn't find much of interest to watch. Nothing really appealed to her. "Guess I'm reduced to watching the news. Aaaagh! Isn't that a sign of old age?

My parents always watched the news. . . she shuddered. . . before that is. I couldn't stand it. . . anything but. . . it's so depressing. Have you ever noticed if you don't watch the news, how the world doesn't seem so bad? But watch the news regularly and you begin to think the end of the world is minutes away. I remember going to see a movie one time called *The Late Great Planet Earth*. I thought it was going to be a science fiction movie – wrong. The movie correlated events in history with foretold occurrences in the Bible. By the end of the movie, I was in a panic. . . all life was over. . . the end of the world was but a breath away. Took me awhile to get over it. Kids are so impressionable.

So, I'm an adult now. I should be able to watch the news without blowing things out of proportion. Who knows, the news may be more like Romper Room compared with all that's been happening around here lately." With that, Jenny sat back to watch the news.

Being a local station, there wasn't a lot of crime talk. Weather, local events – pretty mellow. Then the station went to other news.

There was a special announcement, rather uncommon the news-caster stated. A John Doe had been admitted to the hospital. Due to his condition, the authorities decided to give a general description of the man – what he was wearing, where and what had happened – in hopes of locating a relative or friend. The newscaster continued, ". . . witnesses, and the unfortunate driver of the car, all confer that the man bolted into the street, evidently from an alley way. The driver couldn't stop in time. The accident occurred early this afternoon on Jackson Street, between 3rd and 4th streets. . ."

Jenny gasped, "I was on 3rd today, and I passed Jackson Street just before turning onto Harrison? No, Harvey? Henry! That was it." Her hand gripped the arm of the chair. As the newscaster continued to describe the injured man, Jenny's heart sank. "It's impossible, it couldn't be. . ." She felt sick.

"Authorities ask that anyone with information as to the identity of the injured man contact Memorial Hospital as soon as possible."

"I've got to find out if it is – Jonathan." Jenny, half-tripping out of her chair and raced for the telephone. She picked up the receiver, dialed information, then slammed the receiver back down. "What am I doing? Yeah, get the number for the hospital, call them up and say you think you know who he is? Then when they ask you how you know this man, you just say he's from your dreams. That ought to convince them – that you're crazy! Oh, okay, maybe he didn't actu-ally materialize from out of your dreams, you just dream about him all the time. As if that would clarify matters. No, I have to go there and see for myself, that's the only way." She dropped her hand from the telephone.

"Where's the phone book? I'll get the address from there." Jenny looked like a video-taped mouse in a maze running around on fast for-ward, squeaking, "The book, the book, where's the book?'" Frustrated, she ran back to the telephone, called information anyway, and got the address and telephone number of the hospital.

Within minutes, Jenny was heading back out the door. A chilling breeze clipped her sideways from across the porch, whipping hair into her face – Jenny flashed to the decaying castle – then struggled to pull the strands of hair out of her eyes before she fell down the steps and ended up in the hospital herself.

What a turn in the weather. Jenny pulled her coat tight around her neck as she ran to her car. "Come on Kit, let's get on the road. . . fast!" she implored as she rubbed the dash with one hand, while turning the key in the ignition with the other. You could tell Kit was primed and ready, one turn of the engine and it was purr city. "Release brake. . . into drive. . . and go" as the car flipped a u-ie and zipped down the road.

Clouds were slowly gathering like Raptors for a hunt. No longer white wispy fluffs here and there, but looming heavy – graying steadily, and like the flow of lava – unstoppable.

Jenny felt as if she were moving in slow-motion. She looked at her speedometer a few times, already way over the speed limit, she felt like a snail in peanut butter. Yuck, what a thought.

The air looked thick ahead, kind of fuzzy, then a fine mist began to cover Kit's windshield. "Oh great, lets add some more interference to this high speed mission – rain!" The drops got bigger. Jenny hated driving in rain. She always imagined having to stop fast, putting on her brakes, and just sliding off the road into oblivion, knowing only that wherever she landed, she and Kit would just be some crumpled mess of metal and flesh.

"Stop it, stop it, stop it! You don't have time for this. Caution went out the window the moment you left the house, Jenny. What's more important to you? Huh? You're a good driver, very alert, trust in yourself."

A tree branch flew across Kit's hood and over the windshield. Jenny clamped the steering wheel, not even an atom could squeeze between the two. "Please, go away!" she pleaded, but the rain and wind were unrelenting. The wind began to toy with Kit. A little nudge here, a little nudge there — just enough to keep Jenny on her toes, with a firm grip on the wheel.

Night was weighing heavily as the swollen gray clouds choked the remainder of daylight from the sky. Jenny could feel the depressive nature of the grayness seeping in. In rebellion, she pushed the gas pedal even more.

Chapter 34

The weather outside Memorial Hospital was thick with the threat of an oncoming storm, so also was the atmosphere in the Critical Care Unit with deep concern over the unstable condition of the John Doe patient admitted just hours earlier.

A surgeon in scrubs with the stains of recent surgery dark across his top, was quietly conversing with the elderly head nurse in the hall outside John Doe's room.

"Nurse. I want you to call me if there is any change in his condition."

"Yes, doctor." the nurse responded as they both looked through the door at the injured man lying in the bed.

"Doctor?"

"Yes?"

"What do you think his chances are?"

"It's hard to tell. There was a lot of damage. We repaired as much as we could. Only time will tell now."

"Have you gotten any word as to his identity yet?" the nurse asked with hopeful concern.

"Unfortunately, nothing yet."

They both stood silent for a moment watching the man.

"Doctor, is he coherent at all?"

"It's in and out right now. That's one good sign. Let's hope he doesn't slip into a coma. If he does. . . well. . ." the doctor didn't need to say more. His meaning was all too well understood.

Closing the hospital room door, the doctor looked straight at the nurse, "If *anyone* comes in with information on this man, I want to know A.S.A.P. Is that clear?"

"Yes, doctor," the nurse assured him as he proceeded down the hallway disappearing around the corner back towards surgery.

The nurse took one more look at the injured man through the door window before returning to the nurses' station. There she could monitor his condition along with the other patients in the critical care unit.

"Poor man," she said shaking her head, "someone must surely be missing him. It's times like this you need to have loved ones near. They can make all the difference in the world." All the years she had worked as a nurse, then as a head nurse, she had no doubt that patients fought harder when loved ones were beside them. Too many in her care had just given up when they had to fight alone.

She began to busy herself at the desk, hoping any second the telephone would ring with news of someone answering the newscaster's announcement. Just then, an alarm sounded on one of the monitors.

Chapter 35

*J*enny was never so happy to pull into a parking garage as she was now at Memorial Hospital. She could actually see out her windshield again. Kit no longer had to play the role of the *SeaView*, with Jenny as Captain Crane navigating through blurry waters. Pulling into the garage could very easily have equated to blowing the ballast and surfacing.

She spied an empty parking space and slipped in quickly. "Thanks, Kit. We made it. Take a breather," she said as she patted the dash.

Purse, keys, door locked. . . "Which way?" She panicked, doing a quick 360. "Bingo!" The wall on her right revealed a fairly worn arrow pointing forward towards the elevators. She was off in a flash.

Inside the hospital, Jenny was told she needed to go directly to the Critical Care Unit. The directions the information clerk gave her, led her directly to the nurses' station. Jenny approached the desk.

The head nurse, fiddling with one of the monitors, looked up at Jenny. "Can I help you?" she said with a very non-committal, but somehow intimidating expression.

Jenny was nervous, even feeling a little stupid to think this guy could actually be Jonathan. "I'm here about your 'John Doe' – the one on the news?"

The nurse's expression turned a little leery or defensive – eyes squinting, while her right eyebrow went for higher ground. "Yes? Do you know him? Are you a relative?"

"Yes. . . no. . . I mean maybe, but I'm not sure," Jenny was flustered by the rapid fire questioning.

The nurse frowned. The clicking sound of a pen enhanced the nurse's already agitated attitude. "Which is it? Do you or don't you know the patient?"

Jenny sighed, then took a deep breath trying to draw some extra courage. "I think he could be a friend of mine, but the news report didn't give me enough details to be sure. I won't know for certain until I can see him."

"If there weren't enough details, what makes you think this is your friend?" the nurse prodded.

"Well, because I think I saw him today in that general area, at about the same time." Jenny hoped that would be sufficient enough to satisfy the nurse.

"I don't know that. . ." the nurse began.

Worried the nurse wasn't convinced, Jenny blurted in, "Isn't the important thing right now to find out *who* he is? Continuing with all these questions is just wasting time. I mean, it's possible he's not my friend at all and my information will be totally useless."

"Yes, I suppose so. But we can't just let anyone and everyone see the patient."

"What are you telling me – you've been swarmed with hundreds of people with just as many differed claims as to his identity?" Jenny's eyebrows raised in hopeful emphasis.

"Actually, you are the only one so far."

"Well then?" Jenny said confidently. knowing she had won this round.

"I need to contact the doctor first. If you could just wait here."

"Whatever it takes," Jenny responded, knowing full well that didn't mean staying put to her. She did say, "Whatever it takes," and if that meant checking the rooms before the doctor could come and say no, then so be it.

As the nurse got someone else to cover the station, Jenny slyly began moving around the waiting area, straining her eyes to read the names on the doors closest to her.

"I'll be right back," the nurse assured her. Jenny nodded, smiling sweet as pie.

No sooner had the doors to the Critical Care Unit swung closed behind the nurse, then Jenny turned toward the nurses' station. No one seemed interested in her, as they were busy with their work.

"I've got to do this fast. There aren't too many rooms here, luckily."

Jenny quietly, but quickly moved along the corridor. One, two, three rooms. Then four, fi. . . her breath caught in her throat. She stood frozen.

"Jonathan?" she heard his name, not realizing yet she had said it. She opened the door and moved closer into the room.

He laid quiet, eyes closed. She felt woozy; afraid to walk closer for fear the monitor showing his heartbeat would go flat-line the moment she looked at it. Trying to ignore the equipment, Jenny walked up to the side of his bed, focusing on his face.

"Jonathan. . ." She reached out to touch his face, then pulled back. Instead, she grasped his hand in hers. "Jonathan? Is it really you?" Tears began to well in her eyes. Jenny lovingly looked down at his hand in hers. She squeezed it gently.

Just then, his hand twitched in some recognition. She quickly looked back at his face, holding his hand tightly.

Slowly, his eyes opened. He looked straight at her. Then blinking his eyes as if to clear his vision, his hand clamped hard on Jenny's.

"Jen-ny," his voice strained, "please tell me it's you – that I'm not dreaming."

"Yes, yes, it is me Jonathan, but how. . ."

"I don't know, but I don't care." His eyes slowly closed, then opened again. He struggled against the effects of the medication.

Tears rolled down Jenny's cheeks.

Jonathan swallowed, "Somehow. . . the dreams. . . they must have a reality of their own. I knew my dreams of you were different than my other dreams at night. I could never control the others, but with you, everything was as if in real life, like now. The only thing I couldn't control was your leaving. You'd leave – I'd wake up." Jonathan was about to continue, but stopped when he saw a perplexed look on Jenny's face.

"What's the matter. Jenny?"

"I never dream of you at night."

"What?" Jonathan's face saddened at her response. "I thought I. . . we. . . both of us had the same. . ." Jenny interrupted.

"Of course I've dreamt about you. I mean how else. . ." Jenny blushed, "I just never start dreaming of you at night. It's only during the day, and only when I'm at my special place in the forest."

"I don't understand all this, Jenny" he stopped, his eyes closing for a moment, wincing in discomfort. "Somehow," he began again, as his eyes opened, "you must be the one that's making all this happen."

"Me?" Jenny straightened in utter disbelief. "How could I possibly be? I don't have any control over my dreams!"

"Just think about it. I dream at night. Sometimes the dreams are about you – sometimes not. But you. . . you have to go out of your way to have dreams of me, and they aren't even at night."

Jenny's head was spinning. "Is it possible?" she said without realizing.

"Jenny, think hard. Is there anything else different or unusual you can think of that's happened to or around you that might help explain?"

"Different? Unusual? How about from the minute I got a letter from my aunt, which brought me here?"

"What do you mean?" he said, struggling to keep his eyes open.

"Well, basically, my aunt who swore she'd never leave her house because it was the only thing left to remind her of her only love, ups and gives me the house with no explanation. If that's not enough, I find out no one knows anything. Last person to see her said she disappeared into the forest. . ." Jenny shivered," . . . never to be seen again!"

"What is it, Jenny?" he strained.

"Wait, wait, wait a minute! She always went into the forest. The same place I've been going to – when I dream about you!"

"Huh?" he managed to mutter as he began to cough, not understanding her.

"That funny sensation when I dozed off by the rock. . . the books she'd been reading." It was all flooding in. "My aunt's locket I found in the very same place. The *locket!*" She shouted, reaching into her pocket. "There's a note inside – written to me!" she explained shakily as she fumbling with the clasp.

Jonathan coughed, wiping a trickle of blood from the corner of his mouth before Jenny could notice.

"Here! Here! Listen to this!" She began to read the note again, but Jenny felt as if she was really reading it the first time.

"If to your hand from *clover* lain, this note should find its way. And on this bed of green you stand, have *dreams of love been played.* Then listen well, my child so dear, *they've* heard your *heart*, for *they are here.* A head and heart help *make a whole, not meant to be apart.* There'll come a day, to *go or stay*, for *between you cannot dart. Follow your heart, it knows the way*, so you shall find, what I've found today. Love you forever, Aunt Abbigale." Jenny read with emphasis as the words' meanings took on a new clarity and purpose.

Jenny's heart was beating like never before. "It's all beginning to make sense! I'm here trying to make some logical sense out of my dream love. The *head and the heart*! I now have the same exact health problem that my aunt had. That must have been what she was referring to about not being able to dart back and forth!" Jenny was so excited, she didn't think about what she was saying in front of Jonathan.

Jonathan, now worried more about Jenny's health than his own pleaded, "What do you mean about a health problem? Jenny what is it?"

"Oh, it's nothing. . . really." She hoped the half smile on her face wouldn't give her away. It seemed to work, for the moment anyhow. ". . . a choice to *go or stay*. . . but how? That's why the books, she tried to figure out why, then how. But I didn't find anything useful!"

"Jenny, you're worrying me. You're not making any sense!"

"Wait a minute," she motioned for silence. Her eyes had been darting around as she pictured the events in her head. Suddenly stumped, she fell quiet, looking up with a sad, almost pouting expression.

Trying to quiet another cough, Jonathan grimaced. "What's the matter?" and put both his hands on hers.

Jenny smiled and looked down at his hands. The smile fell quickly from her face – blood. "Jonathan!" her eyes flashed up inquisitively. Jonathan coughed lightly. "What is this?" He lay quietly not knowing what to say. "This is blood on your hand. Where did it come from? Tell me!" she demanded with more tears welling fearfully in her eyes.

"I can't lie to you Jenny, it's not good," he grimaced again. His eyes closed, but they didn't open again. Jenny stiffened.

"Jonathan. . . Jonathan! No, this can't happen. I just found you. Wake up, please!" Unable to hold them back any longer, the tears streamed relentlessly down her face. She took her hand from his and stroked his face – no response. "Jonathan, come back to me," she buried her face in his chest, sobbing.

Then, a hand gently stroked her hair. She jumped up. "Jonathan! Thank God. . .I thought. . ."

"Shhh, Jenny. Listen to me. I don't know how much longer I can hang on."

"No, Jonathan," she cried.

"Jenny *listen*. There's little time."

Jenny wiped her red eyes. "Okay," she managed to squeak out.

"It's up to you now," Jonathan started.

"What do you mean?" she asked with fear in her voice.

"Somehow Jenny, you made it all happen before. We were there! You have to do it again and make it last this time, for both our sakes. Jenny, I don't want to lose you now." Jonathan coughed hard, then swallowed weakly.

Jenny heard commotion coming from down the hallway outside the room. She recognized one of the voices – it was the nurse. . . with the doctor no doubt!

"I told her to stay right here," the nurse assured the doctor.

"Well then, where is she?"

"If she went down to that room I'll. . ." Jenny tuned her out.

"Jonathan! The nurse and doctor are coming. What am I going to say?"

"It really doesn't matter Jenny (cough), it won't make any difference. Not now."

"But Jonathan. . . I don't. . ." Jonathan put his fingers over her mouth.

"They're almost here Jenny. You can't waste time with them, we need all we can get." Jonathan took her hands in his, "You *must* go back and dream, Jenny," his eyes fluttered, "*Dream me alive!*"

Jenny's eyes widened. Jonathan's closed. His hands loosened their grip on hers. Jenny looked at his chest. He was still breathing. They were slow, shallow breaths, but still breathing.

The nurse and doctor were just outside. Jenny jumped up off the edge of the bed, making a fast retreat towards the door. She glanced back once more at Jonathan before she left the room – running smack dab into the nurse and doctor.

"What are you doing here? I told you to wait down the hall," the nurse scolded.

"I'm sorry. I waited. . . but, but it took so long. . . I had to see." Jenny sputtered out.

The doctor put his hand on Jenny's shoulder and turned her attention away from the nurse to him.

"What is your name?" he asked in a gentle voice.

"M-my name is Jenny." She replied trying to ignore the hard glare from the nurse.

"Jenny, since you are already here, tell us, do you know this man?"

Jenny looked at the doctor, quickly trying to figure out how she could explain everything, when she remembered what Jonathan had said about time.

"No, doctor," she said as her eyes lowered from his. " I'm sorry to have wasted your time. But if you'll please excuse me, I have to go now." She tried to convince the doctor, "I still need to find my friend, and it's getting late!"

"Don't worry about wasting my time, I'm just sorry that you didn't know him." the doctor glanced into the room at Jonathan, still lying as Jenny had left him.

"I really must go doctor!" Jenny pressed, as she moved out from under his hand.

"Well okay, no harm's been done," he said looking from Jenny to the nurse, "just be careful out there, the weather let up for a while, but I hear it may turn again for the worse."

"I will doctor, thank you." she said glancing for a moment towards the nurse whose expression did not seem as harsh now.

Jenny was out the door and down the hall. "Hold on, Jonathan." she told herself.

The sky was less menacing as it had been when Jenny arrived. The rain had stopped, but there was still turmoil in the clouds. A breeze clipped Kit broadside as Jenny pulled out of the parking garage.

"Jonathan, please, please wait for me!" she whispered as she headed back towards the Dupree home.

Chapter 36

The doctor and nurse were beside Jonathan. He lay motionless, the only signs of life being the slow methodic rise and fall of his chest, and the all too eerie beep of the monitor.

"Doctor?" the nurse said softly, searched his expression.

"It's not good. He's slipped into a coma. His life signs are getting weaker. I don't expect he'll be in a coma for long, though." They both worked quietly, as there was not much else to say. They just tried to make him as comfortable as they could.

"Maybe it's just as well that Jenny girl didn't know him." His resigned voice falling cold upon the compassion they both felt in their hearts.

Chapter 37

The roads were not welcoming as Jenny sped towards home. She had to make it in time. The wind pushed at Kit from all sides. Headlights whizzed past her. If any of the drivers were to catch a glimpse of her face, it'd probably be enough to steer them off the road. The headlights gave an eerie cast to her already ashen face. Her eyes were fixed, body rigid, as she pushed herself and Kit to the max.

The strain was taking its toll on her. With all her concern for Jonathan, she had forgotten about her own condition. Her body was beginning to remind her of its depleted strength. Luckily, the road ahead was clear of traffic. She couldn't afford to make quick moves, for her mind was turned inward – driving by instinct.

From all the corners of her memory, Jenny was sweeping every speck of information that could possibly help her and Jonathan. "How do I do this? It's one thing to control a situation without knowing, but all of a sudden to have to control it consciously, with life and death (and let's not forget about love), hanging in the balance!"

Jenny bit her lower lip. Eyes glued out the windshield, it was not the road she saw, her vision was filled with the memories of *The Place* in the forest – Aunt Abbigale's strange disappearance, the books, the locket, all swirling endlessly, taunting her, calling her.

The sky was dark and heavy outside. Jenny rolled her window down, breathing in the air, trying to anticipate the weather's intent. Just as she got the window down all the way, a strong gust of wind burst in through the opened gap. Jenny once again was thrown back to her nightmare of the decaying castle. She shuddered – there was an uncanny similarity. Jenny tried to push those thoughts from her mind, but then, she remembered vividly Aunt Abbigale's locket hanging from the door. Some of the fear dissipated. Maybe those nightmares were really trying to tell her something. She ran the dreaded dreams back through her mind. "Aunt Abbigale was trying to tell me something even in those horrid dreams!" The realization began to grow within her. "How could I be so blind? I've always been interested in the meaning of dreams, why have I ignored that interest now?"

Jenny began to sort through all the dreams she'd had since arriving at the Dupree home. "I wish I had written the dreams down. It'd make things so much easier. Too many details are fuzzy," she chewed her lower lip in frustration as Kit charged down the highway through the driving wind and rain. "Okay Jenny, don't try so hard, you'll block everything out. Remember, you heard if the message in a dream is important enough, it'll repeat itself until the message is delivered." With that, the tension in Jenny's face eased. She again was deep in thought. One could almost see the gears moving as she attempted to interpret what she could remember.

Suddenly, Jenny's face went almost ghastly white. With all that had happened up to this point, things were hauntingly clearer. "*The locket!* What it all boils down to, when I was at the castle, I was afraid and didn't know what to do. If it hadn't been for Aunt Abbigale making me find and hold on to her locket, I would have died in that castle!" Jenny gasped, then fell silent for a second, "Something is still missing." Jonathan's face smiled lovingly in her mind.

There was no moon now, the sky was too angry. The wind's strong arms swung at everything in its path, landing the more destructive blows on the trees – their agony seen as the branches fell lifeless to the ground; some voicing one last cry of pain as they hit Kit's body, finally rolling off into the roadway, their needles still twitching in the hungry darkness.

Chapter 38

"Doctor, when the alarm on his monitor sounded, I wasn't sure if. . ."

"I'm glad you paged me as soon as you did. Looks like our John Doe has stabilized a bit for now, for whatever that's worth. Let me know the moment there's any other change in his condition."

"Yes, doctor." the nurse answered solemnly, "Do you think there's a chance he'll pull through this?"

"Nurse, I honestly don't expect him to last the hour. But, we can always hope for a miracle."

The monitor showed Jonathan's heart continued a slow, but notably weaker beat.

Chapter 39

*B*y the time Jenny pulled in front of the house, her nerves were almost shot. Driving up the street had been like an obstacle course. The path constantly changing as anything that wasn't nailed down in the townspeople's yards rolled or flew daringly around her.

This was turning into a bad storm. Even a few surface-rooted trees had toppled over – one forcing Jenny to drive under the end still suspended by the long trunk from which it had snapped in front of her, only moments before.

Now, anticipation of the task ahead wrenched her insides. The moment of truth was close at hand. Jenny's hands still on the wheel, she leaned forward and kissed the steering wheel. "Kit, I love ya. You got me here in one piece. For that fact, you've never let me down. Whoever gets you doesn't know how lucky they are."

Jenny didn't have time for this kind of sentimentality, and she knew it. She got out of the car and ran towards the house – the wind pushing her from behind. She felt like calling for *Toto*, sure at any moment the house would take flight. As she pulled open the screen porch door, for a second she was sure it had been grabbed off its hinges by the wind.

Inside, Jenny pushed against the wind to close the main door shut. Breathing hard, she then turned and pressed her back against the door, standing still in the quiet foyer.

Despair began clawing at her heart. "Not only do I have to figure out how to make this work, but now getting through the forest in this weather, it's horribly dangerous." It took her just the bat of an eye to realize she had nothing to lose, except everything, if she didn't try!

Remembering her sentiment with Kit, she realized going upstairs would be a major mistake. Nothing here but the past with all its fading memories. She had to make every second count.

Jenny touched the heart shaped stone hanging around her neck. "Just a little longer, Jonathan." With that she ran through to the kitchen and was about to go out the door when she thought about the house and lawyers. She raised her head and shouted, "I don't have time for this. . . God please make sure this house is put into the right hands!"

As she headed out the back door, her hand quickly checked to make sure the locket was still in her jeans' pocket.

The wind snipped and howled at Jenny. It must have changed directions, for now it seemed to be pushing against her. She was literally leaning into it, her eyes watering, staggering forward against the blustering gusts – the branches of the forest sentries motioning for her to hurry. The forest's edge never seemed so far away.

Dark and ominous was the forest threshold. A chill of foreboding ran down Jenny's spine as she breached nature's invisible fortress wall.

Jenny began to run – time was slipping away. She had gone no more than 15 feet into the dark woodlands when she stumbled over the root of a tree. Twisting her foot, she rolled over sideways into a batch of nettles. Jenny had no choice but to put her hands down in more stickers, just to be able to get onto her feet. Her injured foot was beginning to swell. She had no time to pamper her bleeding scrapes, for she knew it wouldn't be long before her foot would give out completely.

Overhead, a loud cracking sound. Jenny looked up just as a large branch plummeted towards her. She lunged forward as the branch fell across the path behind her. She got up quickly and didn't stop. Echoing around her were sounds of destruction as the cries of falling trees threatened her chance for happiness.

Jenny had no idea how much time had passed since she'd left Jonathan at the hospital. Neither the rain nor her tears helped her find her way, but she kept pushing on – over, under, around, dodging flying debris.

Just when she thought she'd never find *The Place* in this disorienting stormy darkness, a cold gust of wind caught her attention. She turned and saw the opening over to her left just a few more feet away. Her foot was throbbing, but she ignored it and hobbled a little less quickly.

The Place was no longer pretty and peaceful as it had been before. In the darkness of the storm, it seemed almost void of life. Was she too late? Was this a sign of failure she feared, as she looked around?

"What was that? I swear I saw a couple of flashes over by the rock." Maybe she wasn't too late after all.

Jenny began to make her way over to the rock when her ankle gave out. She cried in agony. "No! Not now! This can't happen now!" She tried to get up. It was no use. Her foot could carry her no farther. She sat and sobbed. A picture of Jonathan's face appeared in her mind.

"You must go back and dream Jenny. *Dream me alive!*" The words pulled at her heart.

"I'm not giving up now!" She shouted at the storm, "I have to get to the rock, that's where I've always dreamt of Jonathan. I can't take any chances, I have to get to the rock!"

With that, Jenny began to crawl, pulling herself over the ground until finally her hands fell upon the soft mossy bed beneath the rock.

Jenny rolled across the moss and sat up with her back against the rock. Leaning her head back, Jenny looked up at the sky. There were no birds playfully swooping in the air, but leaves, branches and twigs tossing around in the relentless wind.

The storm seemed to be out for vengeance as the trees creaked under the stress of its rampage. Jenny reached into her jeans pocket and pulled out the locket. Touching the stone around her neck and half praying, she announced, "This is it, the moment of truth. Jonathan, I need you with me." Then releasing a deep sigh, "Okay, Aunt Abbigale," shouting to hear herself over the raging storm, "I need your help!"

Clutching the locket tight in her fist, head leaning back against the rock, she closed her eyes. "Help me, help me. Aunt Abbigale, pleeeeeease. . . Help me get to Jonathan!" Her head began to ache. She didn't know how to concentrate any harder – wish any harder. She was trying so hard she felt she'd surely burst every blood vessel in her head. Still she tried harder. Still, nothing happened.

Rain now pounding down, mixing raindrops with tears to the point they were indistinguishable. She was queasy and lightheaded from her physical pains. Jenny let out a scream of emotional agony, the physical she tried to forget. A tree on the far side of the clearing fell under the strain of the storm, no longer able to withstand the endless torture.

She tightened her grip on the locket. From her wet palm, traces of pale red streaked down her arm. The clasp on the locket had cut into her hand, but she was oblivious. Instead she raised fisted hands into the air screaming at the top of her lungs, for she knew she was failing, "Jonathan, I'm losing you, help me!" All her energy reserves exhausted, Jenny slumped to the ground, dropping the locket from her hand.

The gut-wrenching sobs of pain and despair continued, but no longer could they be heard above nature thrashing all around her. Now instead of the locket, Jenny hung on to the last little piece of Jonathan – the heart shaped stone.

Even with the driving storm, her limp body could resist the result of fatigue no longer. She began to drift off to sleep.

Faintly, among the moss on which she lay, her voice could be heard whispering, "Jonathan, without you I'm nothing. If I can't be with you, then let the storm take me now." Her last mumbled words before succumbing to sleep, "You have my heart, now take me. . ." Sleep at last.

As the storm came to a crescendo, lightning struck from out of the churning darkness above, splitting what must have been the grandfather of all trees.

Jenny laid motionless clutching Jonathan's stone as one-half of the tree fell across the entrance to *The Place*, and the other half fell like death's sickle across the rock, hitting so hard that what must have been sparks seemed to rise up into the air.

When the tree finally stopped its outcries, there was no sign of the rock, and the moss was completely covered with fragments of the tortured tree.

The storm would not let up for several more hours, but it was of no concern for one man, lying in a hospital bed. The all too familiar haunting sound of the flat line pierced even the sound of the thunder.

Chapter 40

Sparkling, warm, peaceful. A crash could be heard off in the distance, just like her last dream of the castle, when it fell off into oblivion. "It's the same feeling," Jenny thought.

"The flickering, sparkling lights," she tried to focus. "What? Shapes. . . small. . ." she was groggy as if coming out of anesthesia. Jenny couldn't see anything really, just white - and the flickering lights were fading. The white began to take form -- it was turning more into clouds. "I must be dreaming," she thought, as she slipped back into deep sleep.

Jenny roused to the warmth of the sun shining on her face. Dreamily she began to open her eyes. "Blue sky, how pretty," she said with a yawn. Then like a sledgehammer it all came flooding back to her. She jolted up.

"It worked! Thank you, thank you, thank you!" She was alongside the road heading towards Jonathan's ranch. She could see the fence and open gate ahead. Jenny jumped to her feet and ran as fast as she could. Halfway there she realized her foot didn't hurt anymore.

Jenny ran up to the porch and tore open the door. "Jonathan! Jonathan where are you?" She shouted, grinning from ear to ear, but there was no answer. The smile faded. "Oh please!" she pleaded as she ran out of the house, making a beeline for the barn.

The door was wide open. She swung around the stall wall into the open area where Champion had been before. Nothing.

"*Jonathan!*" she wretched out in a sob, falling to her knees. "I'm too late!" Tears streaked her face. "Why?" was all the more she could muster.

Jenny looked around the barn, remembering all the wonderful moments they had shared there together. "What do I do now?" she questioned, feeling fearfully alone and inwardly beaten. The only thing she could do for the moment – *the house.* Mechanically, the body took the uncaring mind back towards the haven where they had found and shared their love for one another. Numb, she dragged herself up the steps to the porch.

"Woof!"

Jenny's head whipped around faster than a spinning top.

"Woof! Woof!"

From the path that led into the field came a familiar sound. Jenny strained, then. . . yes. . . "Champion!" she shouted, practically stumbling off the porch to go to her. With one eye on Champion, her other eye anticipated what she had dared hope for, having just come to believing it was an impossibility.

Champion jumped up on Jenny, her tail wagging excitedly. She hugged Champion who in turn licked her endlessly in the face. Feeling her heart breaking inside, Jenny buried her face in Champion's neck.

"Some people get all the attention!" came a shout from across the yard.

Jenny looked up with blurry eyes, but she didn't need to see clearly to know whose voice that was. "Jonathan?" Jenny wiped her eyes as Champion bounded back off again. "Jonathan!" she tried to say, but it caught in her throat. Within seconds they were in each other's arms. Clinging together so tight for fear it all might disappear.

"You did it Jenny, you did it!" he praised her, as he lavished her with kisses.

"I can't believe it. We made it Jonathan!" she managed between kisses and tears of joy. Just then her grip on Jonathan tightened, "But what if. . ."

He cut her off, now holding her face gently in his hands. "Jenny, you know I was dying. I'm not now. It's different. This time there's no going back."

Somehow, Jenny knew he was right. It was different. She had given her heart and body completely this time, there was no going back, that was gone forever.

With their arms tightly around each other, they slowly walked toward home – Champion bouncing back and forth around them.

"Jonathan?" Jenny shyly began.

"Yes Jenny."

A strange look came across her face, one that he'd never seen before. A twinge of concern spread through his veins. They couldn't have problems after all they'd been through.

"I have to tell you in all fairness."

Jonathan gulped, "What?"

"I'm going to need some. . . *special* accommodations made in the house."

Jonathan's mind was racing, something's wrong and she's trying to ease the blow. "Jenny, what's the matter? Why the special accommodations?"

Seeing the distraught look on Jonathan's face made her giggle. "Oh, you thought. . ." she was going to continue, then decided to spare him. She grasped his hand and placed it ever so gently on her belly. "Well, we can't have a baby without a proper nursery now, can we?" She was positively glowing as she watched Jonathan's shocked response.

"A baby? Oh Jenny, I love you!" He hugged and kissed her like never before.

Champion, aware of the commotion, jumped and barked in excitement. "Life is good Jenny!" he said, as he took her arm and led her into the house.